HER CON
KN

BY
JOANNA NEIL

S & BOON®

DID YOU PURCHASE THIS BOOK WITHOUT A COVER?

If you did, you should be aware it is **stolen property** as it was reported *unsold and destroyed* by a retailer. Neither the author nor the publisher has received any payment for this book.

First published in Great Britain 2004
Harlequin Mills & Boon Limited,
Eton House, 18-24 Paradise Road, Richmond, Su

ISBN 0 263 83936

Set in Times Roman 10½
03-1104-44610

Printed and bound in
by Litografia Rosés, S.A.,

CHAPTER ONE

'JACK, what are you doing out here? Why aren't you in A and E?' Rhianna frowned as she watched her patient making his way purposefully towards the hospital's main exit. When she had last seen him, a few minutes ago, he had been resting on a bed in one of their examination rooms, and she had been confident that it had been safe to leave him in the care of a nurse.

Obviously she had been misguided. She had only left the A and E department long enough to go and get herself a sandwich from the snack bar, and that had been the first break she had managed to grab after being on duty for several hours. They had been so busy this morning that time had just seemed to slip away, and she had been desperate for nourishment. Now, though, it worried her to see Jack Carstairs apparently trying to leave before she had been able to treat him.

'We haven't had the results of all of your tests yet, Jack, and I'm pretty sure that you will need treatment. Please, come back to A and E. It may not be safe for you to go for a while.'

He shook his head. 'There's no point in my waiting around any longer. I feel fine, just a little tired, that's all. Anyway, I only came here because my mother was getting upset and threatened to drag my dad away from the farm if I didn't.'

'Perhaps she had good reason to be concerned.'

'No. She worries too much. I collapsed because I'd been out late last night and I didn't get much sleep. I'm OK, really. There's nothing wrong with me, and I've been away from work for long enough as it is. My boss is already having a go at me for not keeping on top of things. He'll have even more reason to complain if I keep taking time off.'

'You can't help it if you're ill. Your boss will have to take that on board. The preliminary tests showed that there might be a problem, and we need to find out what's causing it.' She gave him a searching look, noting his pale features. His fair hair made him look all the more drained of colour, and he was long and wiry without an ounce of spare fat on him, which added to the impression of fragility. He looked as though he was having a problem holding himself together, and she was sure he was trying to convince himself that nothing was wrong out of a false sense of male pride.

'I thought your brother brought you here,' she said. 'Where is he?'

'He had to go and deal with some things. He hadn't expected to wait around for so long—he said he'll be back later.'

'Then, please, at least wait for him to return.' She reached out to him, gently laying a hand on his arm as though to coax him in the direction of A and E, but just as she did so there was a commotion at the far end of the corridor.

A child, who was around five years old, hurtled towards them, pushing his way past everyone in his path as though he, too, was making a bid for freedom.

Rhianna pulled in a deep breath. Now what? Was the world going mad today? She recognised the boy from earlier that day as the son of a woman who was being treated in the department. The receptionist had been keeping an eye on him, but obviously something had gone wrong and now he was alone, running as though he was in a panic.

'Sam, where you heading off to in such a hurry?'

'I'm going to find my mum. I'm not staying there with that lady.' His mouth was set in a rebellious scowl. 'That man doctor's got my mum somewhere and I want to see her and he won't let me. He's taken her away and I'm going to find her. You're not going to stop me either.'

'It's all right, Sam.' Rhianna used an even, calming tone. The poor child was obviously in a distressed state, and she wanted to do what she could to settle him down. 'No one's going to hurt your mother, I promise you. She banged her head and she's feeling a bit poorly. We want to help her to get better, that's all.'

'No, you don't. That man touched her head and she cried, and now you've taken her away somewhere.' He wasn't going to be pacified, and now he rained blows on her, hitting out wherever he could find a target.

Rhianna bent down to him and held out her arms, wanting to gather the little boy up and comfort him, but he pushed past her and took off once more down the corridor at full pelt.

Rhianna straightened up. Her auburn hair clouded her vision for a moment, and she raked back the mass of wild shoulder-length curls so that she could keep track of him. The child almost ran into a tall man who was walking along the corridor towards them, but the man came to a sudden halt, blocking his path, and Sam skidded to a temporary standstill before veering off into a side passage.

Starting to go after him, Rhianna realised all at once that Jack Carstairs had disappeared. Her shoulders slumped in defeat. He must have taken advantage of the diversion to slip away. She glanced around, but he was nowhere to be seen and she realised that the little boy had to be her priority now. He couldn't go racing off on his own in a large hospital. She needed to find him, and she braced herself in preparation. Things were definitely not going well today.

'Now, you just slow down, young man,' a male voice said, and, hearing it, Rhianna stood still, her mind reeling in shock as she closed her eyes to take it in. It was a familiar voice, deep and satisfyingly masculine, and one that she had not heard in several years. In fact, she had almost begun to wonder whether she would ever hear it again.

She frowned. Bryn? Was it really possible that Bryn was back in South Wales after all this time? The rich tones sounded in her ears once again.

'Things can't be so bad that you have to take off like a rocket, can they? Why don't you come along with me? I'm sure we'll get this sorted out.'

She opened her eyes and there, sure enough, was Bryn, walking towards her, as large as life. Supple and long-limbed, his stride determined, he was exactly as she remembered him, except that now he was holding a wriggling child firmly in his grasp. The boy was kicking out, and she winced, seeing that Bryn was wearing an immaculate grey suit, the jacket hanging open. It wouldn't stay immaculate for long under that treatment, she guessed.

'Bryn?' She was so taken aback to see him that her voice sounded strange even to her own ears. Her heart was pounding, hammering away in her chest so fast that she felt the pulse of it in her throat.

'Rhianna? It's good to see you again.' He smiled, his angular jaw making that captivating quirk that she remembered so well, and she reflected that he hadn't changed a bit—his hair was jet black, cut in a short, attractive style, and he was as good-looking as ever. After all this time he still had the power to make the blood race through her veins. She tried to school her features into an attitude of calm recognition, but it was a struggle, and perhaps she should thank her lucky stars that he couldn't read her mind.

He looked down at the squirming child who was

pinioned against his chest with one arm. 'From what I saw as I was walking towards you, I gather this little fellow has something to do with you? Am I right?'

'Yes.' Her green eyes clouded momentarily. 'I think he was running away because he's worried about his mother.'

'Do you know where she might be?'

Rhianna nodded. She turned her gaze to Sam and stroked his arm lightly in what she hoped was a reassuring manner, but he gave her a baleful stare in return.

'Sam, you really don't need to be worried about your mother,' she told him. 'The doctor didn't mean to hurt her. He was just trying to clean her wound, and now he's taken her to another department to have an X-ray. That will give him a better idea of what damage might have been done when she fell.'

She bent towards the boy in an attempt to get closer. 'An X-ray is like a picture, except that it shows what the bones look like, and if your mother has broken any of the bones in her head the doctor will be able to see. He just wants to help, that's all, and he's doing what he can to make her feel better.'

She wasn't sure whether he believed her, but as she spoke, the receptionist came hurrying towards them. 'There you are, Sam,' she said breathlessly. 'I didn't know where you were and you had me so worried. Your mother's asking for you.'

Sam's eyes widened. 'Is she?' His tone was doubtful and clearly he still felt that they might be trying to trick him.

'Yes, she is. She's just come back from X-ray and she wants you to go and see her. Shall I take you to her?'

He hesitated, turning to Rhianna as though looking for reassurance.

'It's all right, Sam,' Rhianna said gently, as she straightened up. 'You go off with Marianne and see your mother and I'll be along in a little while to check on both of you. Try not to worry. I'm sure everything will turn out well.'

Now that it looked reasonably safe to do so, Bryn set Sam down on the ground and the receptionist held her hand out to the child.

'If you're very good,' she told him, 'you might even be able to have a look at the X-ray. Dr Marston said that there is nothing broken, so that's good news, isn't it?'

Slowly, Sam nodded, and the two of them began to walk back along the corridor towards A and E.

Rhianna watched them go, and then turned back to Bryn. 'That was quick thinking of you to scoop him up the way you did. From the way you took charge of him, anyone would think you were an old hand at looking after children.'

He laughed at that. 'I don't think so. I'd far sooner their parents did that. I'm much too wary to get involved with other people's children.'

His glance shifted over her appreciatively, taking

in the smoothly fitting cotton top and hip-hugging skirt that she was wearing. 'I hadn't expected to see you here today. You haven't changed a bit—except that you're perhaps a touch more frazzled than I remember. You look harassed.' He grinned. 'Is that because of the job? Is this where you've settled these days?'

She winced. How much had he seen of her attempts to get to grips with things? He had never missed much in the past, and she wondered if he thought she wasn't very good at handling some situations. More than likely he thought she was out of her depth.

'It's been a difficult morning,' she acknowledged with a wry smile. 'Yes, I'm working here, in A and E. I certainly never imagined I would bump into you either. It must be more than four years since you were last in South Wales. What brings you back here?'

'My family moved into the area a few weeks ago, and I came down here to visit them. While I'm in the region I thought I would take the opportunity to meet up with some of my former colleagues.'

So he wasn't going to be staying around for long, then. A small drizzle of dejection pooled in her stomach. 'Of course—this is where you did your training, isn't it? I expect you moved on to much better things. What are you doing with yourself these days?'

'I'm working as a locum consultant in a hospital in Clwyd. It's been a good experience.'

She wasn't surprised that he had made the grade of consultant so early in his career. He'd always been determined to get on. He was dedicated to the profession, and he was an excellent doctor. 'I knew things would work out for you. It was what you wanted and I was sure you would make it happen.'

'What about you? How do you like working here?'

'It's good,' she acknowledged, 'but we're rushed off our feet most of the time, especially at the weekends, and we could do with more people in the staff grade posts. Most of the people in the department are under training of some sort. There's a lot of pressure on us and patients sometimes have to wait for quite a while before we can attend to them. It can be difficult, especially if they become restless or irritated.'

Her train of thought brought Jack Carstairs suddenly to mind and she clapped a hand to her mouth. 'Oh, no—I meant to go after Jack, one of my patients, but this business with Sam threw me.'

Bryn's blue eyes widened a fraction. 'More problems?'

She grimaced. 'He was on his way outside and I wanted to stop him. He was trying to leave before we had the results of the tests, and I'm worried about him. If I hurry, I might still catch up with him.'

'I thought I saw you talking to someone before Sam came along to interrupt you,' Bryn murmured. 'He didn't appear to want to stay, and it looked as though his mind was pretty well made up. Are you sure that it's a good idea to go after him?'

'Yes, I'm sure.' Her voice was terse, more so than she had intended. 'I'm sorry—it's something I need to do.' She was torn between staying and talking to Bryn and going after her patient, but in the end her professionalism won out, and she made a half-turn towards the hospital's main door.

Bryn followed her. 'I'll go with you,' he said, 'but, you know, as doctors we can't insist that patients accept treatment. In the end it's up to them to decide what they want to do.'

'I know that, but I have to at least try to persuade him to stay. I'm just so worried that something will happen to him. He was in a bad way when he came in this morning in a state of collapse, and I don't want to be responsible for him having an accident. I would never forgive myself.'

'It shouldn't be your problem.' His mouth made a wry shape. 'But that never made any difference with you, did it? You always did care too much, as I remember it. That's why you got involved with Colin in the beginning, wasn't it? I always thought that was a big mistake.'

'Yes, well, I don't think we'll ever agree on that.' She hurried through the glass main doors as they swished open and he followed her out onto the wide landscaped forecourt of the hospital.

They stood for a moment and looked around. 'I was proved right in the end, though, wasn't I?' Bryn went on quietly, his glance moving over her strained features. 'Colin didn't deserve your help. You always looked for the best in him, but he was an addict who sucked you dry, took everything you had to offer and then threw it back in your face by marrying your cousin.'

'Gwyneth loved him. She was good for him.' She said it with a weary acceptance. In the end even Gwyneth's love hadn't been able to pull Colin out of the mire.

'You were both in over your heads. You dated him for a while, didn't you? I hoped you might come to realise that he had too many problems before it was too late. No matter how I tried to warn you, I could never get you to listen.'

Rhianna grimaced. 'I didn't want to give up on him. I still don't. I would feel as though I was a failure.'

She looked around once more, hoping that she could find Jack. To her left there was a wide swathe of green where the area had been grassed and pleasingly laid out with flowering shrubs. There was a bench where people could sit and take the air, and she hoped she might find him there, but she was out of luck.

She said quietly, 'I think, deep down, Colin's basically a decent person. I've always believed that. It's true that he has lots of problems, but I wonder if things would have been different if his early family life had been stable. Perhaps he wouldn't have messed up if his parents had been around to see him through his troubles. It can't have been easy for him, losing them and going into care at an early age.'

'Other people have similar problems, but they don't turn to drugs and then go on to waste their lives.'

'That's true, but Colin was confused and he has always been easily led. It shouldn't mean that there's no hope for him.'

Bryn's mouth made a sceptical shape. 'I gather from what you're saying that he's still around. I'd heard that he left the area when his marriage to your cousin broke down.'

She nodded. 'He did, but he came back recently. He wants to make a fresh start. He's trying to get his life back together.'

Bryn sent her an oblique glance. 'Knowing you, I suppose that means you're getting yourself entangled with him all over again? I expect you're still doing what you can to get him on the straight and narrow, even now.'

Rhianna felt her skin heat. 'Maybe.' She gave a noncommittal shrug, but Bryn wasn't fooled.

'You never did know how to choose your men,' he said drily.

She turned away from him and scanned the buildings and pathways to the right. He had a point about the men in her life. There had been a time when she had set her heart on Bryn, but she had wasted her time in hoping that he would return her love. That would never happen. He had only ever been protective and brotherly towards her...except for that one occasion when he had kissed her, but that had been a mistake, hadn't it? She pushed the memory away from her.

'Do you see much of Gwyneth these days?' Bryn asked.

She was relieved by the change of topic. 'Yes, we're very close, but she's in hospital at the moment. My father and I are quite worried about her.'

'Oh?' Bryn raised a dark brow. 'What's wrong with her?'

'We're not sure. She hasn't been well for some time and the doctors are doing tests to establish exactly what's wrong. I suspect that she will be in hospital for quite a while.'

'I'm sorry. Does Colin know? Has he been to see her?'

'No. He doesn't know anything about it.' The words came out more quickly than she had meant them to and she tried to soften them now by saying, 'Gwyneth would prefer it if he didn't know. She needs to rest, and she needs peace and quiet.'

In fact, Gwyneth was desperate to keep Colin from finding out anything about her. She hadn't been in touch with him since the break-up of their marriage, and Colin didn't even know that he was the father of a four-year-old boy. Gwyneth was afraid that he would try to get involved with them and, having suffered from first-hand experience of his erratic personality, she was certain that she didn't want a drug addict having anything to do with her son.

'I can understand that.' Bryn looked over to a covered walkway that joined one part of the hospital with another. He lifted a hand to shield his eyes from the glare of the sun, and said cautiously, 'Do you think that could be your patient coming from the hospital restaurant? He looks familiar, from what I saw of him earlier. He looks a bit shaky on his feet. Perhaps we should go over there and have a look?'

Rhianna followed the direction of his gaze. 'You may be right. It does look like him. We'd better hurry—he looks in a bad way.'

The man was stumbling, and as she ran towards the walkway she saw him fall to the ground. Coming closer just a moment or two later, she knelt down beside him and felt for his pulse.

'It is Jack,' she told Bryn, looking up at him briefly. 'I'm barely getting a pulse.' She bent over her patient, and after another second or two she began CPR.

'I'll go and get help,' Bryn said, and moved swiftly away.

Rhianna checked Jack's pulse once more, and said softly, 'Hold on, Jack. We're going to get you back to A and E.'

Jack didn't respond and suddenly went into a seizure, which was frightening to watch, but thankfully it only lasted for just a short time. When he recovered from that, his breathing was deep and sighing, and she checked his pulse once more. It was faint and very slow.

'You're going to be OK, Jack,' she told him, not certain whether he could hear her or understand what she was saying. 'You collapsed because your heart rate was very slow, and for a moment it stopped altogether. That's why you had the seizure. We need to get your heart rhythm back to a reasonable rate.'

Thankfully, Bryn returned just then with the crash team, and between them they carefully lifted Jack onto a trolley. Rhianna gave Jack oxygen and put in an intravenous line.

'OK, let's get him back to A and E as fast as we can.' To Bryn she added, 'Thanks for helping me out this way. You'll have to excuse me, but I need to concentrate on getting Jack's condition stabilised.'

'Of course.'

Once back in A and E, she set up an ECG and began to monitor Jack's condition. 'I'm going to give him atropine,' Rhianna told the nurse who was assisting, but a short time later she realised that the atropine was not having the effect that she had hoped for.

She turned to the nurse once again. 'Would you try to get hold of Mr Bannerman for me, and tell him that I have a patient who is suffering from heart block. Ask him if he'll consider fitting a pacemaker as a matter of urgency? While we're waiting for him to come, I'm going to try external pacing.'

'I'll do it right away,' the nurse said, and hurried away.

Rhianna explained the procedure to Jack, who seemed to be more aware of what was going on now, and he agreed that she could go ahead.

'You were right,' he said, his voice slurred with exhaustion. 'I should have listened to you in the first place.'

'We'll have you feeling better before you know it,' Rhianna said with a smile, 'but I want you to promise me that you'll stay put. I don't want to have to go chasing after you again.'

'Will do,' he managed, and there was even the hint of a wry smile as he closed his eyes in exhaustion.

Rhianna stayed with him until his condition was stable once more, and then she left him in Mr Bannerman's care while she went to check on her other patients.

After everything that had happened, when she looked around she was startled to see that Bryn was still in A and E. He was talking to his former boss, Ross Tennyson, who was still the consultant in charge.

When Bryn glanced in her direction and saw that she had finished working with her patient for the time being, he acknowledged her with a slight wave of his hand. His conversation with Ross came to an end a few minutes later, and he approached her.

'It was lucky for Jack that you insisted on going after him,' he said. 'How's he doing?'

'We've managed to get his heart rhythm back to a more normal state,' she told him. 'I think he'll be all right from here on.'

'That's good. It was strange, seeing him collapse that way and you rushing to his aid—it reminded me of the time when your father had his heart attack. How is Howell? Does he still run the pharmacy in the village?'

She nodded. 'He's doing much better now. If it hadn't been for your quick intervention after the robbery, though, I think he would be in a much worse state these days. The shock of discovering the break-in was too much for him, and I really thought he was going to die. I was in a dreadful state, and I was so relieved when you came in and took over. I didn't know what to do to help him. I felt so helpless. I still dread to think what would have happened if you hadn't been there to save him.'

Bryn shook his head. 'You shouldn't blame yourself. You were only seventeen, and you were as shocked as he was.'

'You were so calm and confident. You knew exactly what to do and I was awestruck.'

'I'm glad it seemed to you that I knew what I was doing,' he said drily. 'As I recall, I'd only just qualified as a doctor, and I was praying that I was doing the right thing.'

'You were wonderful.' She smiled at him, remembering how glad she had been to have him there during that dreadful time.

Ever since then she had worshipped him, and for a long time he'd been unable to do anything wrong in her eyes. She had longed to be with him whenever possible, but then she had gone away to medical school herself and he had moved on to further his career. Their paths had crossed from time to time, over the years, until he had gone to work in Clwyd.

'Do you still live with your father?'

She shook her head. 'It wasn't practical, being so far away from the hospital. It would have meant nearly an hour's drive in peak-time traffic, so I bought a cottage halfway between my father's house and here. It makes life a little easier.'

'I can see that would be more practical.' He glanced around. 'Things seem to have quietened down around here for the time being,' he murmured. 'Is there any chance that we could grab a coffee together?'

'I'm sorry, but I can't. I've already taken a quick break, and I need to check up on my other patients.'

'Perhaps some other time, then?'

'Yes, some other time maybe.' She looked around distractedly. 'You'll have to excuse me, but I need to get on. I have to go and check on some lab tests.'

He looked at her oddly. 'Do I sense that you might be trying to avoid me?'

'No, of course not,' she said, too quickly. He was far too perceptive for her peace of mind. 'It's just that I have so much on my plate at the moment, with visiting Gwyneth in hospital and checking on my father to make sure that he's all right, and we're so busy here. We're often short-staffed and we all try to put in extra hours where we can.'

He nodded as though he understood, but she doubted that he was convinced. He didn't push the issue, but let her back away, and said he'd be in touch. He wouldn't, of course, and, much as she might regret that, she knew that it was for the best in the end. She didn't want to suffer the pain of having her emotions dragged through the wringer all over again. He was only going to be here for a short time, and then he would be heading back up north, and out of her life once more.

When all was said and done, he didn't feel about her the same way that she felt about him, he never had, and it was probably just as well if she didn't see him again.

CHAPTER TWO

'NATHAN, sweetheart, what was that odd little noise that I just heard? Did you bang into something? Are you all right?' A small line indented Rhianna's brow as she looked down at the four-year-old boy who had just come in through the kitchen door.

He looked back at her with a guilty expression. 'I didn't mean to do it,' he explained. 'I was only testing it.'

'Testing what?' she asked. Whatever it was, it sounded like trouble. From his awkward stance and the way he was angling his arms behind his back, she guessed that he was hiding something.

His glance went to the kitchen door, a half wood and half glass design, and as she, too, stared at it, she saw that a faint crack curved along the corner of the opaque window. It hadn't been there before.

'Oh, dear,' she said softly. She leaned over to see what he was concealing behind his back, and then held out her hand for the small hammer which was part of the child's tool set he had been given for Christmas. 'I think you had better let me have that, don't you? It isn't a good idea for you to bang window glass that way. You're meant to use the hammer with the wood that Grandad gave you.'

'I didn't know it would break,' he said defensively.

'Well, now you know what happens.' Her hand was still outstretched, and reluctantly he relinquished the hammer to her.

'Will I get it back?'

'Perhaps,' she said. 'It depends whether you learn how to use it properly or not.'

'I won't do it again,' Nathan promised, giving her a hopeful look.

'Good. I'm glad about that.' She looked at the window and sighed. 'I'm going to have to get someone to come and fix that now.'

Lately, it seemed that there was one problem after another to deal with, especially since she had promised Gwyneth that she would look after Nathan while she was in hospital.

She made a wry face...and yet she guessed that Bryn thought her social life was running perfectly smoothly. She was sure from some of the things he had said that he believed she was footloose and fancy-free, and that she could drop everything at a moment's notice to spend time with him, but he didn't know the half of it, did he?

Turning her attention back to Nathan, she said, 'I think you'd better go and wash your hands before eating. Your plate will be on the table in a few minutes.'

'All right.' Seeing that he wasn't about to get his hammer back any time soon, Nathan looked gloomy, and Rhianna couldn't help feeling a twinge of sympathy for him. It hadn't been easy for him, being separated from his mother, and it must have been a shock for him, watching her being taken into hospital.

Still, he was getting used to living here in the cottage with Rhianna, and she was doing what she could to comfort him and take his mind off things, although neither of them had any idea how long the situation would go on for.

She set the food out on the table, a simple meal of casseroled chicken and vegetables, but it smelled appetising, and her father sniffed the air and commented on that as he came in through the door.

'It looks as though I'm just in time,' Howell Thomas said with a smile. He gave her a quick hug in greeting. 'Just what I need after a day at the pharmacy—a good, satisfying meal.'

He glanced around the bright kitchen, which she had made homely with her own light touch, and smiled in appreciation. 'You know, Rhianna, you've really made something of this place. It's very welcoming. You must be pleased with yourself—you've only been here a few months and you've worked wonders.'

Rhianna smiled. 'I'm happy that it's finished at last.' The pale blue-fronted cupboards reminded her of a summer sky, and she had added a dash of sunshine yellow here and there in the curtains and the tablecloth and in small items of crockery that were displayed attractively on the shelves.

'I'm not surprised at what you've achieved. You had the same creative touch when you lived at home.'

'I'm glad that you liked it.' Some time after her mother had died, she had been conscious that she'd needed to do something to shake her father out of his sadness, and she had set about making small changes here and there to give him something new to focus on.

Bryn had noticed what she'd been doing. He would drop by her father's house from time to time to see how he was doing after the heart attack, and even when Howell had recovered sufficiently to go back to work, Bryn continued to visit.

'I think it's a good idea,' he had said. 'Perhaps if you get your father involved in redecorating. It will give him something to do, something to concentrate on.' He had been right, as things had turned out. Gradually, her father helped out with the bits she'd had difficulty with, and it had given him a new motivation, a new reason for going on.

Now her father said, 'Where's Nathan? Is he playing in his room?'

'I'm here, Gan'pa,' Nathan shouted gleefully, running in and throwing his arms around Howell.

He wasn't his real grandad, of course, but Nathan had always looked on him that way. Before her marriage, Gwyneth had lived with Rhianna and her father, and she had been brought up as part of the family ever since her own parents had died in an accident.

Her father ruffled Nathan's hair, and after a minute or two they all sat around the table to eat.

'Did you manage to look in on Gwyneth today?' Howell asked as he helped himself to new potatoes.

Rhianna nodded. Nathan was preoccupied with making a face out of the vegetables on his plate, and she said quietly, 'After I picked up Nathan from nursery school, we went to see her, but she wasn't really well enough for us to stay very long. They're taking good care of her, but they still haven't managed to isolate the cause of her illness. They've put her on broad-spectrum intravenous antibiotics until they can find out exactly what's wrong.'

Her father grimaced. 'I wish she had gone for help earlier. I knew she wasn't well for a long time and I tried to get her to go and see the doctor, especially when she started losing weight, but she wouldn't hear of it.'

'We both tried,' Rhianna murmured. 'She kept saying that she was just a bit run down and that she would be all right, but at least we know that she's in the right place now. All we can do is hope that they sort out what's wrong.'

'Do you think that Colin will try to get in touch with her?'

She made a face. 'I hope not. She knows that he's back, but she doesn't want to see him and, in fact, I think that's what might have pushed her over the edge. She couldn't cope with the stress of having him around. She said that she couldn't understand how she could have made such a mistake, marrying him in the first place, and I think the last thing she needs is to have him stirring up trouble all over again.'

'I can tell you why she married him,' her father said grimly. 'He put on an act of being charming and caring, and he had her thinking that he was the perfect soul mate. We were all fooled for a while.'

Rhianna winced. She had known Colin since her schooldays, and maybe she understood him better than most people, but her father had little time for him.

'I don't think she ever knew the full extent of his problems,' she murmured, 'or perhaps she thought he'd put them behind him. It was a whirlwind romance and she was swept off her feet for a while.'

'Well, he soon reverted after they were married.' He glanced at Nathan, who was still oblivious of everything around him. 'That little chap was the best thing to come out of that relationship,' he said under his breath, 'but it's a good thing that Colin didn't know she was pregnant when he left her. I dread to think how he would have ruined both their lives.'

Rhianna remembered that conversation with her father when Colin turned up at A and E a few days later while she was on duty. She looked at him curiously, wondering what he was doing there. He wasn't ill, but was just hanging around, and she wondered what he wanted.

'I had an appointment to attend the rehabilitation

clinic here,' he explained. 'They're going to try to sort out some treatment for me, and I just thought, while I was here, it would be good to come and see you. I heard that you had a job here.'

She nodded. 'I've been working here for a couple of years. Is this your nearest clinic, then?'

'Yes. It's quite handy for me. I managed to get myself a flat fairly close to the hospital.'

'I'm glad that you found somewhere,' she said with genuine empathy. She looked him over and saw that he had made an effort with his appearance today. He was wearing smart casual trousers and a freshly laundered cotton shirt, and his dark, curly hair was neatly combed, though a lock of it drifted down onto his forehead. 'I'm sure it will help if you are more settled. How are things going?'

He gave an awkward shrug. 'It hasn't been easy,' he confessed. 'It scared me, having to be treated in hospital after things went wrong with a drug I'd taken. I'm trying to get my life back on track, but it's difficult making a fresh start. I have to find myself a job and get into a routine as well as cope with the withdrawal symptoms.'

She nodded. From what she had heard, while he had been living away he had been taken into hospital suffering from drug-addiction problems and he had almost died.

A phone rang and one of the senior nurses went to answer it. From what Rhianna could overhear of the conversation, she gathered that a child was being brought in by ambulance and would be arriving in around fifteen minutes. She guessed that they would be busy soon in the department.

In the meantime, she scanned Colin's features, looking for clues as to why he was really in A and E. There was a little-boy-lost look about his expression that was oddly endearing, but she had learned to look beyond that.

'I can understand that it must be hard for you,' she murmured. 'The thing is, if you can try to keep busy, you might stand a better chance of getting through your difficulties. I'm glad to hear that you're going to be getting some help.'

He acknowledged that. 'It's a struggle, though. Some days are better than others.' He gave her a searching look. 'I expect you must find that, too, in your job, working here. You have so much responsibility. People's lives are in your hands. I know I was grateful for the skill of the people who saved me.'

He moved a little closer, putting an arm around her shoulders in a cosy, intimate fashion. 'I'm sure that you're brilliant at your job. You were always good to me. You were supportive even when everyone else was against me, and I knew that I could rely you to help me through my bad times. I hope you'll be here for me now?'

'I've always done my best to help you out, Colin,' she murmured, 'and I'll go on doing what I can for you, but this isn't the best time for me just now, you know. I've only just come on duty, and I really need to get on. We've an emergency coming in soon. Perhaps we could talk some other time? I could help you look for a job—there may be one or two people I know who could put in a good word for you.'

He made a rueful grimace. 'I know I shouldn't be here. I didn't mean to keep you from your work. It's just that I hoped you could spare me a few minutes. I've been thinking about you—I wanted to see you.'

A decisive male voice cut into their conversation. 'I'm afraid you'll have to wait until after Rhianna has finished work if you want to spend time with her. She doesn't have time to stand around chatting to you.'

Colin's arm dropped away from her as though she had suddenly caught fire, and a faint look of panic came into his eyes.

Rhianna swivelled round and stared in astonishment at Bryn. He was the last person she expected to see in A and E. More to the point, he was dressed in green scrubs as though he was working here. What on earth was going on?

His gaze was directed at Colin, and his blue eyes held a look that was as sharp as flint. 'We have a patient coming in on a blue light, and we need to make preparations to receive him.'

Colin swallowed visibly, and his skin paled. 'I'm going. It's all right—I didn't mean to get in the way.' He backed away, feeling for the door behind him, and then slipped quickly out of sight into the corridor beyond.

Rhianna stared at Bryn, her mouth tightening. 'Was

that really necessary? You were very curt with him. He didn't mean any harm.' Her brow furrowed. 'Anyway, what are you doing here, issuing orders as though you're in charge?'

His mouth twisted. 'I *am* in charge. As of today, I'm the locum consultant.'

Her mouth dropped open momentarily. Then she shook her head, not quite taking in his words. 'I don't understand. How did that come about? I thought you were working in Clwyd?'

'That was just a short-term contract, and it's over now. I'm sorry if me being here has come as a shock to you.'

He didn't look the least bit sorry. If he had wanted to, he could have given her some warning, and now she said as much to him. 'Why didn't you mention that you might be coming to work here when I saw you last week?'

He shrugged. 'Because nothing had been finalised then. At first I wasn't entirely sure that it was what I wanted and I needed to go through my options with Ross Tennyson. But, as you said, you're short-staffed here, and you can do with all the help you can get. In the end, we sorted things out so that we were both happy with the arrangements. I'm going to be covering the shifts when he isn't around.'

She frowned, absorbing the information. 'I expect that will work out well enough. It's true we've needed extra cover for a long time now, but I hope what happened this morning isn't an example of how you intend to go on.' She glared at him. 'I still think you were high-handed with Colin, unnecessarily so.'

He made a grim smile. 'It's unfortunate that you feel that way, but you need to understand that I want this department to run smoothly while I'm in charge. I'm determined that it will, and that means I'll come down hard on anything that I see as detrimental to the way things go. Colin would be wise to keep away.'

'He wasn't doing any harm. He was only talking to me. Since when was that a crime?'

'I realise that you can't see it,' he said firmly, 'but I'm convinced that he's bad news. He always has been.'

She stared at him. 'What could he possibly do to upset things here? He was behaving in a perfectly reasonable manner.'

'On the surface maybe, but I think that he's playing up to you, winding you around his little finger.'

'Why on earth would he want to do that?'

'Because he knows full well that you have access to drugs, and I wouldn't be at all surprised if that was his ulterior motive in hanging around.'

Rhianna's eyes glittered ominously. She was incensed by that inference. 'Are you doubting my integrity?' she demanded.

'Not at all. It's Colin's motives that I'm questioning. He'll do whatever he can to worm his way back into your life, because he knows that you have a soft spot for him.'

'Why should that be any of your business?'

'It isn't, in itself, as long as he doesn't encroach on your work here, but I can't help questioning what he's up to.'

'Do you find it so difficult to accept that he simply likes me and sees me as a friend?'

He shook his head. 'No, but there's always more to Colin than meets the eye. If we're being honest and bringing things out into the open, I must say that I'm not at all surprised that he still feels drawn to you. In fact, I suspect that you're partly the reason his marriage to Gwyneth didn't last. You and he dated at one time, and I suspect there was far too much unfinished business going on between the two of you.'

She almost gasped at the harshness of that conclusion. 'I have absolutely no idea how you came to believe that,' she said through her teeth. 'It's completely unfounded. I had nothing to do with the break-up of their marriage. I won't stand here and listen to you even imply it.'

He shook his head. 'I'm not saying that you did, intentionally, but Colin has always been interested in you. He may have turned to Gwyneth when you were away at medical school, but that didn't mean that he put you out of his mind.'

Rhianna's outrage flared like searing hot metal. 'I would never do anything to hurt Gwyneth. How dare you insinuate that I would? She's more than a cousin to me—she's like a sister.'

'I know that,' he said, using a reasonable tone. 'I'm not saying that you're at fault. It's Colin that I have my doubts about.'

She pulled in a sharp breath. 'Then I think you should keep your doubts to yourself. I don't see that we can work together amicably if you're going to have an attitude about people I care about.'

'I'm just advising you to be on your guard, and trying to get you to see that it isn't a good idea to have him hanging around while you're at work.'

He said it in a perfectly neutral tone, but she was still feeling edgy. 'You should grant me the courtesy of allowing me to conduct my own affairs the way I see fit.'

It had come as a shock, discovering out of the blue that he was going to be working alongside her, but if he was to be her boss and was intent on being suspicious of every move she made, how was she going to be able to adjust to the situation?

'How long are you going to be working here?' she asked. It could turn out that she was worrying unnecessarily. 'A locum post suggests that it's only temporary.'

He nodded. 'That's right. I shouldn't imagine it would be for more than a few months at the most. Management are keen to try out various ways of providing cover, and this seems to be one alternative. Things may be different later on if regional boundaries change.'

'Is that a possibility?'

'Yes. From what I've heard there could be a big shake-up in the way that facilities are provided.'

That was something, at least. Perhaps, if things turned out for the best, she wouldn't be unsettled for too long.

An ambulance siren sounded in the distance, and they both walked towards the ambulance bay, getting ready to receive their patient. Rhianna sent Bryn a sideways glance. She wasn't at all sure how she felt about him coming back here. He made her nervous and provoked a whole gamut of emotions in her, and she had no idea how things would work out.

'Is there a particular reason why you're taking on short-term contracts?' she asked. 'I would have thought you would prefer something more settled.'

'Not just at the moment. I want to get as wide experience as I can in a number of different A and E departments, so that I can see which strategies work and which don't.'

'But why did you decide on this hospital in the end? Didn't you say you couldn't make up your mind about coming here? Was that because you have worked here before?'

'Partly. I needed to think it through. In the end it seemed like a good idea because things have changed since I did my training here, and it looks as though there will be new challenges. Added to that, my parents are living in the area, so it will give me the chance to see more of them.'

She nodded. 'I see. I expect your family will be glad have you around.'

'Even if you're not?' He sent her a wry smile, but there was no more time for talking after that because the ambulance was drawing up, and maybe that was just as well. She was feeling too shaken up to have a rational conversation with him. They hurried to meet the ambulance.

The paramedics brought out a stretcher, and their patient, a child of around five years old, was quickly transferred to a trolley. Together, they whisked him into A and E.

'This is Josh Walker,' the paramedic said. 'He was involved in a road traffic accident. He's suffered a head injury, and his level of consciousness deteriorated on the way here. We've been giving him oxygen and he's had medication for the pain.'

The little boy was in a bad way, with an open head wound, and it grieved Rhianna to see him like that. He looked so small and vulnerable that her heart went out to him.

Bryn took charge right away. 'I'm going to intubate and ventilate,' he said, beginning to secure the child's airway, and then went on to check him for any other injuries.

Rhianna put in an intravenous line and set up a drip to replace the fluids that had been lost. Because he had an open wound he would also need antibiotics to ward off any infection.

She watched Bryn at work, and was thankful that

he was looking after the boy. He was gentle yet thorough in the way he examined him, and she knew instinctively that the child was in good hands. It was always nerve-racking to have to tend badly injured children, but Bryn's quiet, calm manner instilled confidence in those around him. He was efficient and experienced, very sure about what needed to be done.

'OK,' he said a few minutes later. 'We've done what we can to stabilise him for the time being. Now we need to get a CT scan.' He turned to Rhianna. 'Will you keep the parents informed?'

She nodded. They must be desperately worried about their little boy, and she would do what she could to allay their fears.

'Mr and Mrs Walker?' she said a few moments later. 'Would you like to come into the waiting room? I'm here to answer any questions that you may have about Josh.'

They were both white-faced and distraught because their child was hurt. 'He ran out from behind a parked van,' the boy's mother said in a distressed voice. 'I called after him to stop, but he wasn't listening. The car driver tried to brake, but he was too late, and there was nothing he could do to avoid him. I felt so helpless. It was awful.' Tears trickled down her cheeks and she dashed them away with the back of her hand.

'We're doing everything we can to take care of him,' Rhianna said softly, 'but we'll need to admit him for observation. We'll be monitoring his condition the whole time, and we'll keep you informed of any changes.'

'Thank you,' the father said. 'I'm sure you're doing your best for him.' His voice broke. 'He's all we have. Seeing him like that—so defenceless—it's unbearable.' He pulled in a gulping breath and tried to rein in his anxiety. 'How long will it be before we have any news?'

'These things take time,' Rhianna answered. 'It's difficult to say right now, but his condition appears to be stable for the moment. Once he's more responsive we'll know.'

She did what she could to put their minds at rest and answer their questions. They were shocked and anxious, and she felt their anguish as though it were her own.

'If there's anything you want in the meantime—a cup of tea or coffee—you only have to ask. I'll hand you over to a nurse who will look after you. As soon as there's any news, I'll come back and talk to you.'

Rhianna went back to the treatment room a few minutes later, and it was only then that the trauma of the last half-hour hit her. It was one thing to do her job and make sure that everything was being done to save the child's life—after all, that was what she was trained to do and she did it automatically, almost without thinking—but, somehow, facing the parents and dealing with their torment had been a far more difficult challenge this morning.

Perhaps it was because their son hadn't been much

older than Nathan, and she knew how devastated she would be if anything happened to him.

Bryn was examining another patient's X-rays, but now he glanced at her briefly. 'Are you all right?' he asked.

'Yes, of course. Why do you ask?'

'You look a bit shaken. It's never easy, coping with small children who are hurt. I know you're a fully fledged doctor, a senior house officer, but you haven't worked in Emergency all that long, and it can be very stressful, especially when your patients are very young.'

'I'm fine. There's no problem, really.' She hesitated a moment, then said, 'I sometimes think that dealing with parents can be one of the more tricky parts of the job. There's no sure-fire way to tackle the situation and make everything all right. They are so traumatised, and it's hard to know what to say that will make them feel any better. Basically the only thing that counts is to be able to tell them that the child is recovering, and that isn't always the case.'

She pulled a face. 'I suppose I'll get used to it in time, but I can't help wondering how I would feel if it was my own child who was injured.'

He glanced at her curiously. 'You always wanted children, didn't you?'

She nodded. 'It's only natural, isn't it? Don't you want children of your own?'

He was thoughtful for a moment. 'I'm not sure…certainly not for a while yet, because there are so many things going on in my life just now. Later, possibly.' He grimaced. 'Anyway, I'm not sure how good a parent I would make. I haven't had many dealings with children—normal, healthy children, that is.'

She looked at him questioningly. 'You have nieces and nephews, though, don't you…your brother's children? Hasn't being with them given you some idea of what it might be like?'

He shook his head. 'They're still very young, and I haven't seen a lot of them lately. Perhaps that will change now that I've moved back into the area. I'm not sure that being with them will give me a taste for parenthood, though. I don't seem to have the ability to bond with other people's children very well. It's a flaw, I know, but I've always been glad to hand them back at the end of the day. They can seem like too much hard work when they get up to mischief.'

'I've never felt that way.' Even though Nathan could be hard to handle at times, she loved him to bits.

Bryn studied her, his gaze slanting over her features and then going to her hands. 'No. I can imagine you with a family of your own. I had almost expected to come back and find that you had married, but you're not wearing a ring.'

'Things don't always work out the way we think they will, do they?' She was silent for a second or two, reflecting on what might have been. 'Anyway, I've been busy building up my career, and marriage has been the last thing on my mind.'

Besides, there had only ever been one man she wanted, and he wasn't interested. She looked at Bryn now, and wondered what it would have been like if he had shared her feelings.

There was only one time that she had dared to hope, but that one summer evening when he had kissed her was a long time gone.

They had met up at the house of a mutual friend, she remembered, where there had been a celebration party and they had danced out in the garden, swaying to a slow, sweet melody on the patio beneath the star-studded sky. They had both drunk more than a little wine, and it had been late in the evening. She had been startled when he had asked her to dance, but it had been a heady experience, being held in his arms, and she had wished that it would never end. And when he had kissed her it had been as though all her dreams had come true.

But then the music had stopped and he had put her away from him, gently but firmly, and had looked down at her as though he had regretted what had happened.

'I'm sorry,' he said, with an odd little smile. 'I shouldn't have done that. I don't know what I was thinking. Put it down to too much wine and moonlit madness.'

A few days later he went away, to take on a post as registrar in a far-away hospital, and for a time she felt as though her heart was breaking, as though she had lost someone special, and she knew that her life would never be the same again.

In the distance, another siren sounded, bringing her back to reality. 'Another patient coming in,' Bryn said, efficient and authoritative once again. 'Let's get organised, folks.'

Rhianna made an effort to push the past behind her and switch her mind back to the present. It was time to get back to work, to deal in practicalities. There was no point in dwelling on what was over and done with.

Bryn had never shown that he felt anything more than affection for her, and that wasn't likely to change. Now he was here as her boss, and she was going to have to find a way of working with him.

CHAPTER THREE

'WHAT are you going to play with today, Nathan?' Rhianna asked, ushering the little boy into the hospital crèche.

Nathan was frowning. Nursery school had closed for the summer, and she had been lucky to get him a place here, but he wasn't reacting all that well to the change.

'Don't know,' he said. He hunched his shoulders in a diffident gesture, and she looked at him in concern. It troubled her that he was having problems adjusting. What could she do to help him to settle?

'Let's take a look around, shall we?' she murmured.

For herself, bringing him here made things easier all round where work was concerned, except that she was constantly anxious in case they ran into Bryn or Colin.

There was always the worry that if Bryn were to see them together, he might start asking questions about who Nathan's parents were, and she wasn't sure that she was ready to face those just yet.

If Bryn discovered the truth he might inadvertently let it slip to Colin, should they bump into each other, and then there would be trouble, because Gwyneth didn't want him to know anything at all.

She could ask Bryn not to say anything to him, but he might not agree to keep it quiet. Despite the fact that he wasn't certain he wanted children of his own just yet, Bryn had always been adamant that parents had a responsibility to their offspring. He might even feel that, despite Colin's problems, he had a right to know about his son, but no one could be certain how Colin would react to the news.

It would be different if Gwyneth was well enough to deal with the inevitable fallout but, as things were, Rhianna found herself treading a cautious line.

Looking at Nathan, she couldn't help feeling anxious for him. These were early days yet at the crèche, and he was finding it difficult to cope. It had been hard enough for him to accept his mother's illness, and now he seemed a little quiet and withdrawn.

'There are lots of toys set out on the tables,' Rhianna pointed out. 'I can see jigsaw puzzles on that one, and some construction blocks on the one over there. What would you like to do?'

Nathan hesitated, but he was perceptive enough to know that he had to make a choice of some sort.

'Jigsaws,' he answered after a moment or two in a low voice. He didn't seem too sure of himself. His thumb was in his mouth, and he was hanging back a bit.

'I thought you might choose those,' Rhianna said, putting an arm around his shoulders and coaxing him towards the table where a group of children were already seated. 'You've always liked doing puzzles, haven't you?'

She waited while he sat down. He looked around at the other children, not saying anything, until one of the boys leaned over and pushed a jigsaw piece into his hand. 'You can do this one with me, if you like,' the child said. 'I don't know where that bit goes.'

Nathan responded with a shy smile. His shoulders lost some of their stiffness, and he stared at the assortment of pieces with his new friend.

Watching the children study the puzzle together, Rhianna began to relax a little. Perhaps things would work out after all.

'You can leave him with us,' the nursery assistant said with a smile. 'I'm sure he'll be fine, but if there is a problem of any sort I'll give you a ring in A and E and you can perhaps come up and talk to him. You don't need to worry.'

'Thanks. He looks as though he's more settled now.' She bent down and gave Nathan a hug and a kiss, and said, 'I'll come up and see you in a little while, chick, when I get a break.'

He nodded, and then turned back to the puzzle.

Rhianna made her way towards A and E for the start of her shift. It had been a bit of a rush this morning, but as things had turned out she still had a few minutes to spare and there would probably be enough time for her to go to the snack bar and buy a pack of sandwiches for her lunch later. It would save time in the end and allow her to spend longer at lunchtime with Nathan. With any luck, she would be able to pop in and see Gwyneth, too.

As she stood in the queue, waiting to be served, she was startled to see Colin come in.

'I thought I caught a glimpse of you in here,' he said. 'I didn't think we would meet up with each other for a while, so this is a bit of luck, running into you this way.'

Rhianna wasn't so sure about that. She felt a sudden quiver of alarm ripple through her veins. She had been anxious about Bryn coming across them, but it hadn't occurred to her that Colin would be around this early in the day. It was just as well that she hadn't met up with him a few minutes ago when she had been with Nathan, wasn't it?

'What are you doing here at this time of the morning?' she asked.

'I'm attending the clinic here. Remember, I told you they were going to arrange some rehabilitation sessions for me?'

'Yes, I remember. I didn't realise they would start before breakfast-time.'

'I'm a bit early,' he confessed. 'I was feeling a bit restless and on edge, thinking about it, so I thought I would come and get myself a cup of coffee first.'

She gave him a brief smile. 'Actually, I suppose I wasn't sure that you would go through with it.'

He didn't take offence. 'It was one of the conditions I signed up to when the flat was made available to me.' His mouth quirked fleetingly. 'They might throw me out if I don't keep to the bargain.'

'Are you finding the rehab difficult?'

'It isn't too bad. I have to see a doctor and talk with him for a while, and he does blood and urine tests to make sure that I'm keeping on the straight and narrow. There's a lot of checking up, but my counsellor said she thought it would help me to get back on my feet. I'm being given a new start, if you like, away from all the influences that were in my life before.'

'So the offer of a flat is meant to help with that?'

He nodded. 'That's right.'

'It's probably a good idea,' she agreed. 'What are the people like in your neighbourhood? Have you made friends with any of them yet?'

'They seem to be all right. There are a couple of lads who are both out at work during the daytime, and there is a young woman who has a toddler at home with her. She's divorced, but I don't think she has much contact with her ex. I think that's probably a shame, because the little boy looks as though he could do with a father figure around.'

'Oh? What makes you think that?'

He shrugged. 'Nothing in particular. It's just that he looks a bit wistful sometimes, and he watches the kids playing football on the green as though he'd like to join in. Their dads mostly take them along.' He made a grimace. 'I know what it's like to have no father around, and I know that if I had a son, I would want to be with him. I wouldn't like to be kept out in the cold, the way Steph keeps her ex away.'

'Perhaps she has her reasons.' Rhianna lowered her head momentarily. She had guessed that he might feel that way, but she didn't think that it would be sensible for him to know about his own son, given his background of fecklessness and unreliability. He might be making an effort now, but until he had proved himself fit Gwyneth would not want to tell him about Nathan.

She looked up and saw that the snack-bar assistant was ready to take her order. Picking out a pack of sandwiches from those on display, she handed over the money.

Turning back to Colin, Rhianna said, 'I have to rush off now and get to work, but before I go, I have something for you.' She rummaged in her bag and drew out a sheaf of folded papers. 'I was hoping I would bump into you again so that I could give you these. They might be useful to you. I've spoken to some people, and they've given me the names of a few companies where the management is fairly sympathetic to people who want to make a fresh start.'

He took the papers from her. 'That was good of you,' he said with a smile. 'Thanks, Rhianna. Perhaps I'll give them a call.'

She left the snack bar a moment later, and made her way towards A and E. In the corridor, she almost collided with Bryn, who was heading in the same direction, and coming across him like this just a minute or two after her meeting with Colin gave her nervous system a sharp jolt.

She came to a swift halt and almost overbalanced, but he reached for her, steadying her, and she felt a warm flush of heat wash through her body as his hands curved around her upper arms. His hands were strong, yet gentle, his long fingers lightly restraining her. Her heart started to hammer in her chest.

'Hey…slow down. We're not in a race. You're not on duty for another ten minutes yet.'

'Is that right?' she said with a nervous laugh. 'I seem to be losing track of time this morning, with one thing and another.'

He let her go, and her pulse gradually began to settle to a more normal rhythm. 'I saw you talking to Colin just now,' he said, the timbre of his voice deepening. 'You look a little bit edgy. Perhaps he's the reason you're out of sync.'

'Did you?' Another tremor of alarm shot through her. She shook her head, the bright auburn curls tumbling about her shoulders. 'If I'm edgy I don't think it's because of anything to do with him. I was in a hurry, that's all. Colin and I just happened to run into each other. He's attending the rehabilitation clinic here, so that shows he's serious about making a recovery, doesn't it? He told me that he wants to get his life sorted out—with a new flat, a new job and so on. He's making an effort, isn't he?'

'It looks that way, doesn't it?' He didn't sound convinced, and she sent him a quick glance.

'Don't you think rehabilitation works?'

'I didn't say that. I'm sure if someone is determined enough, if they've reached a low point in their lives and they want to put all the bad things behind them, it's possible to make a complete recovery, with help. They need to have the will to do it, though, and I'm not sure that Colin has the staying power to see it through.'

'I think you're misjudging him. He'll make a go of it, I'm sure he will.'

He grimaced. 'He's lucky to have you to believe in him. Not everyone is so fortunate to have someone who cares standing by. I just hope he doesn't let you down.'

She searched his features curiously. 'When did you become so cynical?'

Bryn returned her stare, his blue eyes cool and steady. 'I'm not cynical. I'm a realist. I've seen what addiction can do to people. It takes hold of them, and quite often they turn to crime to fund their addiction. I know that's what almost happened to Colin in the past.'

He frowned. 'It isn't always easy for people like him to go back to living a normal life. You tend to overlook that. You prefer to live with your head in the clouds, in a world where everyone is good at heart and those who have strayed can be brought back to the fold. I think you're fooling yourself, but if it makes you feel better to think that way, who am I to disillusion you?'

He sounded so sure of himself, but Rhianna wasn't swayed by his incisive, matter-of-fact manner. She wasn't going to let him fill her head with doubts. She had known Colin before he had become addicted to drugs, and she remembered his youth and uncertainty, and how troubled he had been, and how much she had wanted to help him through his difficulties. Bryn was less sympathetic, and he couldn't see beyond the man he had become.

Watching Bryn later, though, when they were working together, it was clear that despite his somewhat sceptical outlook on life he was a man who could be depended on. He treated everyone who came into A and E with the same level of compassion and care, no matter what the circumstances. Seeing him in action helped to lift her spirits.

It was a particularly difficult day. There was a bad road traffic accident early on, and when they had finished dealing with the casualties from that there was a spate of minor injuries to keep them busy.

A woman brought in her next-door neighbour, a younger woman who was complaining of chest pain and breathlessness. There was a child with them, a little girl who was being comforted by the older woman.

'This is my neighbour—Lisa,' the woman said. 'She was taken ill this morning, and I could see straight away that she needed help, so I brought her here as fast as I could, in my car. Can you do something for her? She's finding it really hard to breathe and I'm very worried about her.'

'I'll take care of her,' Rhianna said. She turned to her patient and called for a nurse to assist. It was clear that Lisa was in pain and that she was finding it difficult to stand without assistance, but even so she tried to disguise what she was feeling and managed to put on a brave face for her child.

'Let's see if we can make you comfortable in the examination room, Lisa,' Rhianna murmured. 'I'll check you over and see if we can find out what's causing your problem.'

'Mummy...Mummy...' The child's voice called to them as they moved to the examination room. It was a distressed, wailing sound that tugged at Rhianna's heart.

'That's my little girl,' Lisa said, her voice rising. 'What's going to happen to my little girl?' The woman began to panic, and Rhianna gently tried to soothe her, knowing that the stress was not doing her any good. Her breathing was coming in short gasps and Rhianna could see that she was in a lot of pain.

'Is that your little girl, with your neighbour?'

Lisa nodded. 'Her name's Charlotte. I need to know that she's going to be all right.'

'We'll make sure that she's being looked after,' Rhianna promised, 'and we'll bring her to be with you again as soon as I've examined you. It's probably for the best that she doesn't come with you just now, because it might be frightening for her to see you like this. Could we contact her father?'

Lisa shook her head. 'I don't want him near her,' she said breathlessly. 'He left us.'

Rhianna saw that she was wearing a wedding ring. 'But you are still married to him, is that right?'

'No, we're divorced. I don't want you to get in touch with him.'

'All right. There's no need for you to be upset, we won't worry about that right now. Let's get you onto a trolley.' She gestured to a nurse. 'Emily,' she said softly, 'will you help me for a moment and then go with Lisa's neighbour and the child and look after them? Perhaps you could find the little girl some toys to play with.'

Emily nodded. 'I'll see what I can do,' she said.

Rhianna turned back to her patient and with Emily's help settled her on a bed. 'Try not to worry. We need to concentrate now on helping you to get better.'

Rhianna checked Lisa over. She was generally feverish, which suggested the possibility of an infection of some sort, and Rhianna ordered blood tests. She was concerned about her condition, though, and the level of breathlessness, and asked softly, 'Are you experiencing any other symptoms?'

'No. Except…' The woman seemed to be confused. She frowned. 'My leg… I had a bad pain in my leg. I didn't know what—' Suddenly, it seemed to be all too much for her, and she slumped sideways, appearing to collapse. Worriedly, Rhianna checked her vital signs.

'What's happening here?' Bryn came to stand beside her, and she felt a flood of relief flow through her. One moment her patient had been sitting up and talking to her, and now she was in a really bad way. It helped to have Bryn there. He gave her confidence that between them they would do whatever they could for her patient.

'She suddenly collapsed and her heart's racing. She complained of leg pain, and I'm worried about the possibility of a deep vein thrombosis. There may be complications from that.'

He nodded. 'It's possible that you're dealing with a pulmonary embolus. You can confirm that later with the person who brought her in. It could turn out that she's been on a plane journey recently. In the meantime, you need to get her on oxygen quickly and do an ECG. Give her 10,000 units of intravenous heparin as a bolus over five minutes, and then start a continuous infusion at 1000 u/h. You should treat the arrhythmia, too.'

'I will. As soon as I've done that, I'll get a chest X-ray and refer her for an urgent ventilation/perfusion scan.'

Rhianna was desperately worried for her patient. It was no wonder that she had been concerned about her little girl. She must have guessed that something was dreadfully wrong. Now, Rhianna was working frantically to save her life.

'Are you OK?' Bryn asked a short time later. He must have sensed how shaky Rhianna was feeling inside. She had tried not to let it show and had concentrated on helping Lisa to the best of her ability, but the little girl was at the back of her mind the whole time, tearing at her consciousness.

She shook her head. 'She has a daughter…a little girl aged about three. I'm so worried for both of them. If only I could have seen Lisa earlier perhaps I could have prevented this.'

'You're doing the very best you can,' he said calmly. 'Nobody can ask any more of you than that.'

'What if it isn't enough?' she asked in a despairing voice.

He said quietly, 'Along with everything else, you've put in a central line, and you're giving her saline…and you're dealing with the arrhythmia. Have you notified the intensive therapy unit?'

'Yes, I've done that. I'm waiting for Mr Bannerman to come down and look at her. I've asked him to consider doing an emergency pulmonary angiography.'

'Then you've done everything that you can for the time being. All you can do now is to wait for results.'

Mr Bannerman approached as they were talking, and Rhianna reluctantly relinquished her patient to the surgeon's care. She felt an intense need to be with the young woman, as though she could in some way instil the will to fight in her. Her child needed her. She had to win through.

'Come on,' Bryn said firmly. 'It's time to take break.'

'I don't need a break,' she said, resisting his efforts to turn her away from the examination room. 'I have patients to attend to.' She couldn't bear the thought of anyone else going into a relapse before they could be examined properly.

'No, you don't. Everything else can wait. There are other doctors who can take over.' He laid a hand on the small of her back and urged her towards the doctors' lounge.

The lounge was empty, a peaceful oasis in the chaos of the emergency department. Rhianna felt certain that she shouldn't be in there, but Bryn held her by the shoulders, his strong hands keeping her still.

'Take a few moments,' he said. 'Take some deep breaths. You'll soon feel better.'

She had no choice but to do what he said. He wasn't going to let her go, so she grudgingly conceded defeat, dragging air into her lungs, shakily at first and then with more surety.

'How do you feel now?' he asked. He was looking at her steadily, scrutinising her features for any sign that she was still feeling weak.

'I'm fine, really. It was silly of me, I suppose, but I just hate the thought of anything happening to her and the little girl being left alone in the world.'

He frowned. 'Isn't the father able to help out?'

'I don't know,' she admitted. 'Anyway, Lisa doesn't want him involved.'

He shrugged. 'She may not have any choice. Fathers have rights, too.'

'I know.' She braced herself. She had always known his views on that topic. 'I'm sorry for giving in to my emotions that way, for letting you down.'

'You haven't let anyone down. You're only human, Rhianna. This can be a horrendous job sometimes. It can be heartbreaking, but you mustn't let it get to you or you'll not be any use to any one. You're a good doctor. You need to remember that.'

'Thank you.' She gave him a faint smile. It was good to know that he respected her on a professional basis. 'I'll be all right now. I'll go back to work.'

He shook his head. 'No, you won't. Not yet. Go and pour yourself a cup of coffee. When you've had ten minutes, you can come back and see more patients.'

The door to the lounge opened and a nurse put her head around it. 'Bryn, we've a heart-attack patient coming in. Two minutes.'

'I'm on my way.' He turned back to Rhianna and pushed her gently down into a chair. 'Coffee,' he reminded her. 'I don't want see you back in A and E until you've done as I say.'

'Yes, boss. Anything you say, boss.'

He sent her a mock glare of admonishment, and then went out of the door.

As soon she had finished her coffee, she went back to work. He had been right, she acknowledged inwardly, she had needed to take time out to calm down. The break had done her some good, and she felt more able to face things now.

Bryn was busy attending to the heart-attack patient, and there was no opportunity for her to talk to him again. She concentrated on dealing with her own patients over the next hour or so, and when there was a lull in the proceedings, she took the opportunity to take her lunch-break and go and see Nathan in the crèche.

He was perfectly happy playing with his friends, as it turned out, and after she had eaten lunch with him she left him to go on with his afternoon activities.

There was still time for her to go and pay Gwyneth a quick visit. She hoped her cousin wouldn't be upset at not seeing Nathan, but she didn't want to disrupt his day too much.

'How are you feeling today, Gwyneth?' Rhianna sat beside her cousin's hospital bed a few minutes later, and held her hand.

She looked around the room and saw that Gwyneth's condition was being monitored by a variety of equipment, and she was receiving medication through a drip. 'Has the pain eased at all?'

'A little,' Gwyneth answered softly. 'They're giving me painkillers.' She moved restlessly against her pillows, her fair hair tumbling around her cheeks. 'How is Nathan?'

'He's fine. He's settling down at the crèche, and I didn't want to upset his routine by bringing him here in the middle of the day. I'll bring him in to see you later today.'

'Thanks. I can't wait to see him. I hate being stuck in here and not able to look after him myself.'

'You mustn't worry about him,' Rhianna urged her. 'He's making friends at the crèche, and he said he wants to make a card for you to help you to get better. I'm doing my best to explain things to him as we go along, and he knows that you're going to be here for a little while.'

'I wish I knew how long that was going to be. The doctors have tried to explain to me what was wrong, but I couldn't follow everything they said. They're treating me with antibiotics, but I don't think they're working too well. I heard one of the nurses say that they're barely keeping the infection on hold. I don't think they've found the exact cure just yet.' She paused to take a breath as though the effort of talking had been too much for her. 'Have you been able to speak to the doctor?'

Rhianna nodded. She could see that Gwyneth was exhausted from just talking, and it made her anxious to see her so ill. 'He said that you have had an infection which has been rumbling away for some time, and it has affected your heart. They're doing tests to try to isolate the particular bacterium responsible, and as soon as they have the answer they will be able to give you a treatment that's tailored for the condition. In the meantime, it's important that you rest and try not to worry about things.'

Gwyneth made a faint smile. 'I don't seem to have much choice at the moment.' Her expression sobered. 'I heard that Colin is back in the area. He's planning on staying here.'

'Who told you that?'

'A friend who came to visit me.' She sent Rhianna an anxious look. 'Have you seen him?'

Rhianna nodded. 'He comes here to the hospital because he's going through rehabilitation. I think he's trying to get his life back on an even keel.'

'He's tried that before, but then he got back in with his friends and there were times when he disappeared for days. He would turn up again the worse for wear. I don't believe he can do it.'

She began to look agitated all at once. 'He mustn't know about Nathan. I don't want him to know about him, especially while I'm stuck in here. He'll try to get custody of him, I know he will, and I don't trust him to take care of him. He'll pretend to the authorities that he's doing all right so that he can get his own way, and Nathan will end up confused and upset.' Her blue eyes were wide and frightened. 'Please, don't let him find out, Rhianna. Promise me?'

Gwyneth was looking distressed, and Rhianna was worried that she would suffer a relapse. 'I won't tell him, I promise.'

'But if he sees Nathan with you, he'll ask you about him. What will you say?'

'I could say that I'm looking after him for a friend.'

Gwyneth shook her head and sank back against her

pillows, overcome by the effort. Her fair hair was slightly damp now from faint beads of perspiration that were breaking out on her brow. It curled in soft tendrils over her forehead.

'He'll ask questions. He might link him back to me, and he might wonder about the likeness between himself and Nathan unless you put him off the trail,' she said distractedly. 'Couldn't you say that he's your child?'

Rhianna thought about it. 'Other people might want to know what's going on. How can I suddenly produce a child and say he's mine?'

Gwyneth tried to straighten up. She moved restlessly against the white pillows and Rhianna was struck by how pale she looked. 'You could say you felt bad about being a single parent. It's only for a little while, until I'm back on my feet. Then you can tell everyone the truth. Please, Rhianna…will you do this for me?' She paused to pull in a shaky breath. 'I know you think Colin isn't so bad underneath, but he can be devious. He was always underhand when he was on the drugs. He'll try to pull the wool over people's eyes.'

Bryn had said something similar, and Rhianna felt torn. 'I don't know if I can make it work. Nathan might give the game away.'

'He might not. He calls you mum-mum, as it is.' Gwyneth managed a small smile. 'He never did manage to say Rhianna.' Her eyes pleaded with her. 'Say you'll do it for me, please?'

Rhianna felt herself relenting. It would just be a small deception, wouldn't it? Once Gwyneth was well again she would be in a position to tell Colin the truth.

'If it will make you rest easy, then I'll do it,' Rhianna said at last, 'but you have to promise me that you will stop worrying. It isn't doing you any good at all, and I want to see you getting your health back from here on.'

'Oh, thank you, Rhianna.' Exhausted, Gwyneth slumped in the bed.

A nurse came to take her temperature and pulse, and looked at her with a frown. 'You've been getting upset,' she said. 'We can't have that. You need complete rest.' She directed a stern look at Rhianna. 'It's very important that she stays calm. You should go now. I think she should try to get some sleep.'

'I know. I was about to leave anyway.' She stood up and looked at Gwyneth. 'I have to get back to work, but I'll come and see you later, with Nathan. Everything will turn out for the best, you'll see.'

Gwyneth gave her a wan smile, and Rhianna left her in the care of the nurse, who was still showing her disapproval.

The rest of the day went by in a flash. They were busy in A and E, but Rhianna found time to check up on two of the patients that were worrying her.

The little boy who had been injured in the car accident a while ago was responding to treatment at last, she discovered. It was good news, and it made her feel brighter.

'You're looking more cheerful,' Bryn commented, coming across her by the desk. 'It's good to see you smile. What's brought that on?'

'Do you remember Josh Walker, the boy we treated the other day? He's on the mend. I've been worried about him, but from the sound of things he's going to be all right.'

'That's great news. His parents must be over the moon.'

'I'm sure they are.'

'How's your patient from this morning doing—the woman with the pulmonary embolism?'

Rhianna frowned. 'She's in Intensive Care, and she's stable at the moment. They have her on thrombolytic therapy and we're hoping for the best. Her neighbour is taking care of the little girl in the meantime.'

'Let's hope she pulls through.' He glanced around the department. 'Things look quiet for the moment. Are you going off duty now, or do you want to grab a coffee with me? We could talk, and catch up on a few things.'

'I'd like to stay,' she said apologetically, 'but I really need to get home. Perhaps we can catch up another time?'

'Of course.' He sounded as though he accepted her reason, but his expression was slightly guarded and she wondered if he thought she was being evasive. There was nothing she could do about that, though.

She had to go and collect Nathan. He was her first priority.

She took Nathan to see his mother, but the nurse who had been on duty earlier was still determined that Gwyneth should get as much rest as possible, and their visit was a very short one.

'Mummy's tired,' Rhianna explained, watching Nathan carefully as they walked towards the car park. 'She needs to have a little sleep, but she's happy now that you've been to see her. She loved the card that you made for her, didn't she?'

He nodded, and gave a little smile. 'I cutted out some pretty flowers and sticked them down. She said they was beautiful.' He ran over to Rhianna's car. 'Can I make some butterfly cakes for Mummy when we get home? She likes those.'

Rhianna smiled wearily. 'Yes, all right, if you like.' Baking was the last thing she wanted to do after a full day at work, but it was something he had enjoyed doing with his mother, and if it would make him happy then she would go along with it.

'That man's looking at you,' Nathan announced. 'Do you know him?'

Rhianna turned to see who he meant, and her heart gave a little jump when she saw that Bryn was standing just a few yards away by his car. He was looking at her with an arrested expression, his gaze travelling from her to Nathan.

'Yes,' she said to Nathan. 'I know him. I work with him.' Rhianna unlocked the car and ushered the child into his seat. 'Let's get you fastened in, shall we? You can look at your book on the way home.' She made sure that he was secure in his seat and then handed him a picture book.

Closing the car door, she turned to see that Bryn was coming towards her.

'Now I see why you had to rush off,' he said in a level tone. 'Is he the reason why you rushed off at lunchtime, too?'

'I didn't know you had noticed,' she said uneasily.

He made a half-smile. 'There isn't much about you that I don't pick up on,' he murmured, 'but I must say this is something I hadn't expected. Is he yours?'

She hesitated for a moment, wondering how she should answer. If she told him the truth, could she rely on him not to tell Colin? All in all, she didn't think so.

Hadn't he always said that he believed in fathers having rights where their children were concerned, even if they were absent fathers? He might decide that, since he was undergoing rehabilitation, Colin had every right to know about his son, even if he didn't completely trust the man.

In the end, she reasoned, she owed it to Gwyneth to keep her promise to her. But the deception bothered her.

'Why should it come as such a surprise to find that I might have a child?' she prevaricated. 'These things happen.'

She comforted herself with the fact that she wasn't

telling an outright lie. Nathan was her responsibility right now, and if anything happened to Gwyneth she had promised that she would take care of him.

Bryn was shocked, that was clear to see. 'It just didn't occur to me,' he said, with a vague shake of his head, as though he was trying to clear it, 'especially after you said that you weren't married.'

His glance went to her left hand as though to convince himself that he had his facts right. 'You didn't marry the father?'

She shook her head. 'No.' Now he had even more reason to be fazed by the discovery.

Nathan was beginning to fidget inside the car.

'Look, I'm sorry, but I have to go,' she said, thankful for an excuse to make her escape. This was turning out to be much more difficult than she had expected. 'Nathan's getting restless.'

He nodded, and made no attempt to stop her from leaving. His blue eyes followed her as she went around to the driver's side and he watched her as she pulled open the car door. His expression was stunned, as though he was still having difficulty taking it in.

Rhianna started the engine and tried not to imagine what he was thinking. She had made her decision and gone along with what Gwyneth had asked her to do. Now there was no going back. She could only hope that she didn't come to regret it.

CHAPTER FOUR

'HOW long has the child been in this condition?' Rhianna asked the nurse who was assisting her. She was examining a little girl who had been brought into A and E by her parents, presenting with high fever and back pain, along with episodes of vomiting. It was distressing to see her looking so frail and ill.

'She started to feel unwell a few days ago, apparently,' Emily said, 'but her parents thought she was suffering from a tummy bug. It seems that to begin with her symptoms weren't as bad as this, but she's gone rapidly downhill in the last few hours.'

'Poor little scrap.' She wasn't much more than five years old, and Rhianna could see that she was in a lot of pain. She tried to be gentle as she examined her, but the little girl writhed uncomfortably and Emily did her best to soothe her, wiping her brow with a damp cloth.

'I'm sorry if I'm making you uncomfortable, Chloe,' Rhianna said softly. 'Just bear with me a little while longer—I need to find out what's causing you to feel so poorly.'

To Emily, she added, 'We'll need to collect a specimen of urine and do a dipstick analysis. I'll need a blood culture as well. I suspect that she's suffering from a kidney infection, and I'm worried that she's already beginning to be toxic.'

Bryn appeared in the examination room a little later as Rhianna was preparing an intravenous infusion of antibiotics. She hadn't seen him to speak to him this morning, as he had been involved in treating the victims of a boating accident, but she hadn't been sorry to put off talking to him. She had been off duty for a couple of days, and this was the first time she had worked with him since the evening when he had seen her with Nathan.

'What's happening here?' he asked.

'I'm treating Chloe for suspected pyelonephritis,' she told him. 'I'm giving her replacement fluids along with antibiotics and analgesia for the pain.'

He frowned, checking the little girl over briefly. 'She's showing signs of septicaemia,' he said. 'We need to act quickly. Are you making plans to admit her?'

'Yes, I've already made arrangements for that. I'm just hoping that the antibiotics will stop the septicaemia before it takes hold.' Rhianna made sure that the child was being given oxygen and that her condition was being monitored before she left her in the care of the nurse.

'She doesn't look very much older than your little boy,' Bryn said as she went to write up the child's case notes. 'How old is he—three, four?'

She had desperately hoped that he wouldn't bring up the subject, but it wouldn't have been likc him to avoid the issue, and now she pulled in a quick breath and answered, 'He's just four years old.' She was going to have to think on her feet if he began to probe too deeply.

'I only saw him for a short time as you were walking to your car, but he looks a lively little fellow. He seemed to be chatting to you happily about something or other.'

'He was telling me about his day at the crèche and asking me if we could bake cakes. He enjoys cooking with me, but it can be a messy operation.' She smiled, remembering the way they had both ended up covered in a fine dusting of flour.

'It must be difficult for you, coping with a child, especially when you work full time.'

'It can be, yes,' she admitted, 'but it has its compensations. There are times we share together that are precious.'

Her mouth indented as she thought back to the evenings when she had sat and read a book with Nathan on her knee, and he had fallen asleep with his head on her shoulder, his warm little body curled up against hers. He looked so innocent and vulnerable then, and she realised how deeply she cared for him. It also made her acknowledge to herself how she sometimes ached to have a child of her own.

'Even so, how do you manage to fit it all in? There must be times when your arrangements fall through, or he's ill, perhaps?'

'I've not had too many problems so far. My dad

helps out sometimes, when he isn't at the pharmacy, and it's good for Nathan to have a man around.'

Bryn looked at her thoughtfully. 'Isn't the boy's father living with you?'

Rhianna averted her gaze. 'No.'

'Why is that?' Bryn asked softly, his gaze narrowing on her.

'It just hasn't worked out that way,' she told him. She began to reach for a patient's chart, hoping that he would take the hint and go and attend to his own work, but he stayed determinedly by her side.

'But he is part of Nathan's life, isn't he? He must have some contact with him, surely?'

'No, he doesn't.' Bryn had always been persistent in getting to the bottom of things. She ought to have known this would be no different. She said, 'He doesn't know about Nathan. He left before he was born.'

Bryn's eyes widened. 'Have you never been in touch with him to let him know?'

She shook her head. 'It's better this way.'

He frowned. 'I can't believe that you're saying this. How can it be good for a man not to know that he has a son?'

'Let's just say that there are reasons why it's best he doesn't know.' She studied the chart in front of her, but it might have been written in a foreign language for all the sense it made to her just then. 'I ought to get on,' she said in a low voice. 'I have patients to attend to.'

He brushed aside her evasive manoeuvre. 'Nobody here has ever mentioned your child. Is that because you've kept it quiet from them, too?'

'Yes,' she said quickly, suddenly nervous that everything would begin to unravel, 'and I'd rather you didn't say anything to them either. I prefer to keep my private life to myself.'

He was frowning deeply now, and she realised with a sinking feeling how entrenched she was getting in this deception. If only she hadn't made her promise to Gwyneth... This could all get rapidly out of hand.

'Isn't that an odd way to handle things?' he persisted. 'Surely, you need all the support you can get? Or are you afraid that something will go wrong and the father will find out about him?'

He stared at her, his eyes glittering as recognition dawned on him. 'That's it, isn't it? He's likely to come back and he'll want to know what's going on.'

He was getting too close to the truth for her peace of mind, and she said brusquely, 'These are my problems, Bryn, not yours. You've been away following your own career for a long time, and I've been used to handling my own affairs without interference. I don't need your input now. My relationships are my business, not yours.'

It was a brutal, blunt way of putting it, but she didn't see any other way of making him leave the matter alone. It was hard for her to deceive him this way, and her only comfort was that she hadn't told him any deliberate untruth. She could only justify her actions to herself by knowing that he had reached his own conclusions from what she had said.

He looked at her searchingly, and she was afraid that he was going to ask more questions, but instead he nodded briefly and began to check his own list of patients. 'As you say, it's your business. Who am I to interfere?'

He didn't mention the subject again, and as the day progressed she gradually began to relax a little. After work, she took Nathan to see his mother for a brief visit.

He chatted to her brightly for a while, and then amused himself with the toys that Rhianna handed to him. Gwyneth was happy to see him, but she was tiring quickly and Rhianna cut short their stay as soon as she saw that it was getting to be too much for her.

Nathan, luckily, was blissfully unaware that his mother's condition was deteriorating, but Rhianna wanted to know more about what was happening and stopped to have a word with the nurse before they left.

'She isn't doing too well, is she?' she asked. 'Can you tell me what's wrong with her? Are you any nearer to finding a specific treatment?'

'The doctors have tried several different treatments, but so far none of them has been powerful enough to stop the infection in its tracks. I'm afraid that she has developed a heart murmur, and that's giving us some cause for concern.'

It was bad news, but Rhianna was glad that Nathan

had no inkling of how ill his mother was. She took him home, and later that night, when she had settled him down in bed, she couldn't help wondering what was to happen. Gwyneth had to get well. Nathan needed her. They all needed her to get well.

In the morning, Rhianna woke with a muzzy head and a sick feeling in her stomach. At first, she put it down to anxiety about Gwyneth, but by the time she had put breakfast on the table for Nathan, she realised that she was coming down with some kind of stomach bug.

There was no way she could get into work or cope with taking Nathan to the crèche, and as a last resort she rang her father and asked if he could help out.

'Of course I can help,' her father said. 'I'll do whatever I can. Give me half an hour, and I'll be with you. He can stay with me for the day, and I'll ask my assistant at the pharmacy to keep an eye on him.'

He hesitated for a moment, thinking things through, and then asked, 'What about you? How you going to manage? Should I call a doctor to come out and see you? Do you need someone to come and stay with you?'

'No, I'll be fine. It's just Nathan that I'm worried about.' It made her uneasy to realise that this was the kind of situation that Bryn had pointed out. There were pitfalls to looking after a child when you had sole responsibility.

'All right. Keep your phone by the bed and I'll

check up on you every now and then. Perhaps you'd be better off staying at my house.'

'Thanks, Dad, but I'll be all right here. I don't have the energy to make the move right now. As soon as you've collected Nathan, I'll go back to bed, and with any luck I'll be right as rain by tomorrow.'

She called the hospital and told them that she was sick and wouldn't be coming in to work, and shortly after that her father arrived to collect Nathan.

The boy was happy to be with his grandad, and she knew that he would be in safe hands.

As soon as she had waved them goodbye, she hauled herself upstairs to the bathroom. It wasn't a good day. She felt wretched. In between bouts of vomiting, she lay in bed, and it wasn't until much later on in the day that she began to feel a little stronger.

In the evening, she settled into a warm, sudsy bath to try to ease her aching limbs. It was blissful to lie back and relax and let all her cares float away, and it wasn't until some half an hour later that she climbed out and reached for her towel.

The doorbell rang, disturbing her haven of peace, and she gave a heavy sigh. Who could that be at this hour? She really didn't feel up to having visitors.

It could be her father, of course, with Nathan. He had said that he would take him to see Gwyneth when the pharmacy closed, and he may have decided to look in on her on their way home.

She slipped her arms into her towelling robe and

fastened it around herself before going to answer the door.

It wasn't her father. Bryn stood on the doorstep, and for a moment she couldn't quite take it in that he was here at her cottage. He was dressed in casual clothes, olive-green chinos and a paler green cotton shirt that was unbuttoned at the throat. He looked good, heart-warmingly attractive, and he was altogether too much for her fragile nervous system to cope with right now.

'May I come in?' he asked, his voice deep and mesmerising, smoothing over her senses like dark chocolate.

She tried to pull herself together. Just looking at him made her feel weak, and had her senses leaping about all over the place in utter chaos. 'Of course. How did you know where I lived?'

'I looked you up in the phone book. You're the only Thomas listed in this village, so I was pretty sure I had the right address.'

She realised that she was keeping him standing in the hallway, and she suddenly remembered her manners. 'Do you want come through to the kitchen? I'll put the kettle on. I expect you'd like a coffee?'

'That would be good, thanks, but perhaps I should make it. How are you feeling? When you rang in sick today, I was worried about you.' He looked at her closely. 'You're very pale. Should you be up and about?'

'I'm feeling much better now, thanks. It's one of

those twenty-four-hour things, I imagine. I've been sick a few times but I think I'm OK now.'

They had reached the kitchen by this time, and Bryn looked around appreciatively. 'This looks good. I imagine that window makes it very light in here earlier in the day and the colours are bright and cheerful. Was it like this when you moved in, or have you done all this yourself?'

'The units were pretty much the same as they are now, but I've added the tiles and a touch of paint. I've only been here for about six months, so there are still parts of the cottage that need to be redecorated. It's just a question of finding the time to get around to it.'

His gaze shifted to a toy car that had been left on the kitchen worktop. 'I expect you have enough on your hands, with looking after Nathan.'

Her stomach gave a lurch as she remembered that he thought Nathan was her little boy. She nodded. 'That's true, but I suppose I'll get there in the end.'

'Is he in bed? How have you managed to look after him today? I couldn't help wondering how you were going to cope.'

'He's at my father's house.'

'Ah, that's good. I thought you would perhaps have made arrangements for him to go somewhere else. I remember you said Howell looked after him sometimes.'

He glanced around once more, looking for the kettle and then he took it over to the sink and filled it with water. 'Are you having coffee?'

She shuddered at the thought. 'No, thanks. I think I'll just stick with plain water for now.'

'Can you manage anything at all to eat? I can make something for you, if you like.'

She shook her head. The mere thought of food still made her queasy. 'Not for me. Have you eaten yet?'

She glanced at the kitchen clock. 'You must have come here straight from work.' He had taken the time to change out of the suit he usually worc, though. He must keep a change of clothes handy at the hospital, she guessed.

'I did. I live in the next village to this one, so I thought I'd look in on you as I was passing through.'

'That was thoughtful of you, but I'm fine, really.' Having him here in her kitchen was making her nervous all at once. It had been so long since she had seen him outside the work situation, and it was suddenly overpoweringly intimate to have him standing at close quarters in the confines of this small room.

'I wasn't expecting anyone to call in on me,' she added hastily, 'and I feel bad about putting you out. You work long hours as it is, and I hate to think I've kept you from your supper. Can I get you something to eat?' She needed to be busy, to stop herself from succumbing to the chaotic flurry of her senses.

'No, Rhianna,' he said, his tone serious. 'That's not why I'm here, for you to wait on me. I really think you should sit down and let me look after you.'

He was watching her closely, and she was sure he must be able to see the flush of heat that raced along her cheekbones. 'You say that you're all right, but you look as though you're about to fall down any minute. Sit down. Let me take care of you.' His glance wandered over her, sliding down over the towelling robe she was wearing and coming to rest on the bare expanse of her legs.

She clutched the robe around her, suddenly anxious in case it should come adrift. 'I don't need you to take care of me,' she began, but he ignored her feeble protest and gently cupped her shoulders in his palms and pushed her down into a seat.

'Do as you're told,' he said. He laid a hand on her forehead and murmured softly, 'You're still feverish. I'll get you some water.'

He filled a glass with ice-cold water and handed it to her. She sipped at it gratefully, aware that her hands were shaking a little. She tried to still them. If she was feverish it was because of him, she thought distractedly. She could scarcely think straight with him around, and he made her unnervingly mindful of her state of undress.

What had seemed like a perfectly sensible towelling robe earlier on now seemed to cover far too little of her. She was all too aware of the nakedness of her throat, and of the way the fabric persisted in sliding off her knees to reveal more of her legs than she cared to show.

'Relax,' he said. 'I'm not about to leap on you.

Even I can see that you're not well.' He grinned at her, and she was suddenly conscious of how perfectly masculine he was, of his attractively sculpted features. They were enough to set any woman's heart pounding.

He turned away from her to prepare a mug of coffee, and when he had finished and had seated himself opposite her, she found her pulses were racing all over again.

As a distraction more than anything, she murmured, 'You said that you were living in the next village—have you bought a house there or are you renting?'

'I'm renting a property,' he said. 'I'm not sure how long I'm going be in the area, so it wasn't worth looking for a permanent place. It's only a small house, but I'm happy enough where I am for the time being and the rent is reasonable enough. I'm within twenty minutes' drive of my parents' place and my brother's, which is what matters most.'

She had almost forgotten that he wasn't going to be around for very long. The reminder came as a bitter blow. She could get used to having him near, but she realised it would be foolhardy to hope for too much.

The thought made her sad, and it must have reflected in her expression because he said quietly, 'I really think you ought to be in bed, you know. You may be feeling better than you were earlier, but you still don't look fully recovered. I think you need to rest, and the best place for that is in bed. I'll help you up there, shall I?'

She shook her head. 'You don't need to do that. I can manage.' He was right, though, she didn't feel well, and perhaps it was the shock of seeing him here that had sent her into a downward spiral. 'Perhaps I will go and lie down for a while. Do you mind? I'm sorry to be such dismal company.'

She got to her feet, swaying slightly as the room seemed to swirl around her. A fog suddenly enveloped her mind and she couldn't think clearly at all. Perhaps she had stood up too quickly.

She didn't remember falling, but in the next few moments she was vaguely aware of being gently held, cocooned by strong arms and reassured by the steady thump-thump of a heartbeat beneath her cheek.

'You'll be all right,' she heard him say, though his voice sounded muffled to her ears. 'I've got you. Everything's going to be fine.'

After that, the world seemed to slip away, and she was floating on a soft cloud, enveloped in a warm nest of downy comfort.

She didn't know how much time had passed, but when she woke she was bemused to find that she was in her own bed, tucked up in the folds of her quilt, and bright sunshine was trying to poke through the curtains at her window.

She squinted at the curtains, trying to recall how she had come to be here, but the memory evaded her.

'You're awake, then.' Bryn's voice reached her

from across the room, and she opened her eyes wide to take in his long, rangy frame. What was he doing here?

Confused, she asked, 'Is it morning? How long have I been asleep?'

'All night,' he said, with a smile. 'You were feverish and I gave you a couple of paracetamol to bring your temperature down.'

She didn't remember that at all, and now she frowned.

'How are you feeling now?'

'Better,' she said, realising that it was true. She felt as good as new. There was no aching in her limbs, and she moved her shoulders, stretching to enjoy the sensation of well-being.

A waft of cool air drifted over her bare skin, and she clutched the quilt to her in sudden dismay, until to her relief she discovered that her modesty was not necessary. She was perfectly decent beneath the covers. She was still wearing her robe, but it had somehow fallen from her shoulders to reveal a wide expanse of creamy flesh.

Bryn's mouth made a faint quirk as though he recognised her dilemma, but he simply said, 'Good. Perhaps you could manage some breakfast. Some toast, maybe, and some cereals?'

She nodded. 'That sounds great.' Her brows met. 'Were you here all night?'

'Yes. I didn't like to leave you while you were ill.'

She looked him over, but he didn't look at all crumpled and she wondered where he had slept.

'I slept on the sofa,' he said, interpreting her uneasy look. 'I came to check on you from time to time, but you were sleeping peacefully once your fever broke.'

He walked over to her and placed a tray on the bedside table, and she saw that he had laid it with tea and biscuits. 'Just in case you woke feeling famished,' he murmured. 'You've not eaten over the last day, and I don't want you fainting from hunger.'

'That was thoughtful of you.' She gave him a little smile. 'Thank you for staying with me—but I feel awful, thinking that I must have put you out. I'm sure you have other things you could be doing. You shouldn't be wasting your time here with me. You must be—'

'It was no trouble.' He cut her protest short. 'I had absolutely no intention of leaving you while you were in that state.'

'But you—'

She didn't get the words out. Unexpectedly, he bent down to her and kissed her swiftly on the mouth, stemming the tide of her misgivings. He gave her a brief smile. 'I'm glad you're feeling better.'

The kiss was over almost as soon as it had begun, and she stared up at him in startled bewilderment. What had that been all about? Her lips still tingled as though he had lit a fuse inside her, but he was acting as though it was nothing. Perhaps it wasn't, to him.

More than likely, he had kissed her because he wanted to stop her from voicing her doubts.

He said lightly, 'You had me worried there for a while. I can't have my best senior house officer going down with the flu. How would we cope?'

He was teasing her, but his words brought her back to reality and she said cautiously, 'What day is it?' Then added, with growing alarm, 'I should be getting ready for work.'

She started to push away the quilt, and made to swing her legs out of bed, but he stopped her, his hand firmly steadying her. It was perhaps just as well, because a wave of dizziness washed through her head momentarily. It was lack of food, probably.

'No, you don't. You stay in bed and take things easy. You'll be no good in A and E if you're still recovering from a bug and, anyway, your father rang while you were asleep and said he's going to stop by and see you later on this morning. He said to tell you that Nathan's fine and he'll drop him off at the crèche.'

'You two seem to have sewn things up between you,' she said with a lift of a finely arched brow.

'We certainly have.' His manner became brisk and matter-of-fact. 'I'll bring your breakfast up here, and then, unfortunately, I shall have to leave, because I do have to put in an appearance at work. I don't expect to see you there until tomorrow at the earliest.' He directed a stern look her way in case she was thinking of putting up an objection.

She spread her hands, palms upwards in a gesture of defeat, and he chuckled and went out of the room.

A few minutes later, he brought her breakfast up on a tray and then left her to it with a brisk admonition to stay put.

She heard the front door shut a short time later, and she lay back against her pillows, feeling as though she'd been flattened by a whirlwind. She still had no clear idea why he had kissed her, but the memory of it was there inside her head like something to be preciously guarded. He would laugh if he knew how much it meant to her.

Of course, her first thoughts on the matter were most probably the right ones. He had probably simply intended to shut her up. To him it had been a brotherly gesture, a way of saying that he was glad she was well, but it meant nothing more than that. She was kidding herself if she hoped that it might.

CHAPTER FIVE

'HOW are you feeling, Gwyneth?' Rhianna looked anxiously at her cousin. She was very pale, and struggling to get her breath.

'I'm not doing too well today. They say they need to check my heart over.' Gwyneth paused, giving herself time to rest. 'The doctors say they are going to do an…echo—something.' She looked as though the thought of it worried her.

'It's called echocardiography,' Rhianna hurried to explain. 'It won't hurt at all. The doctor will use ultrasound to show the heart at work, and the pictures on screen will enable him to see the chambers of the heart and the valves and so on.'

Rhianna guessed that the infection which was laying Gwyneth low might be causing a problem with one of the heart valves, and that was why she now had a serious heart murmur, but she didn't want to add to Gwyneth's worries by telling her this.

'I wish I could beat this thing,' Gwyneth sighed. 'I'm so worried about Nathan. I want to be with him.'

'Of course you do,' Rhianna said in a sympathetic tone. 'I'm sure things will change for the better soon and you'll be back home. He talks about you a lot, you know, and he can't wait for you to be with him.

If it's any consolation, at least he seems to have settled down with me for the time being.' She was doing her best to put a positive gloss on things. It alarmed her to see Gwyneth looking so down.

'I feel more secure about things, knowing that you're looking after him. Colin's still around, though, isn't he? Remember, he mustn't find out about Nathan. I'm sure he'll try to claim custody, and that mustn't happen.' Gwyneth was beginning to look agitated, and Rhianna hastened to reassure her.

'You mustn't worry about that. I won't let it happen, I promise.'

Gwyneth sank back against her pillows. 'I will get better, won't I?' she said, struggling to get her breath back. 'This can't go on for ever.'

'Of course you will.' Rhianna said it with conviction, but inside she was feeling very anxious. Gwyneth's treatment was not going well, and from what she had learned from the nurses, the antibiotics had not had the effect they had hoped for.

'The important thing is that you get as much rest as you can, and you must try not to worry.' She glanced briefly at her watch and winced. 'Look, I have to go back to work now but I'll bring Nathan in to see you later when he finishes at the crèche for the day. He looks forward to spending time with you.'

Gwyneth smiled. 'I love to see him.'

Rhianna hurried back to A and E. The waiting room was full, but in the examination room she saw that Bryn was talking to a boy who was around eight years old. The child was pale-looking, almost as though he was in a state of shock. Bryn appeared to be trying to comfort him, and Rhianna wondered what had happened.

'You were very brave, Tim,' Bryn was saying. 'You did the right thing, calling for an ambulance, and now we're doing everything that we can to help your father to get better.'

The boy looked upset, and Bryn gave him an encouraging smile and put an arm around him in a gesture of friendship. 'Is there someone that we can call, someone who can come and look after you? Your mother, perhaps?'

The boy shook his head. 'My mum's gone out,' he said. 'I don't know where she is. I was staying at my dad's house for the weekend. I tried to phone her but she didn't answer.'

'Do you usually live with your mother?' Bryn asked gently.

'Yes.' He chewed at his lower lip for a moment or two. 'My dad was supposed to take me to the cinema, but we didn't go. Some friends came to see him.' He was beginning to get upset all over again, and Bryn gave his shoulders a quick squeeze.

'It's all right, Tim, you don't need to worry yourself. We'll see if we can find your mum for you. If you go along with the nurse, she'll look after you and perhaps she might be able to find you some games to play with while you're waiting.'

Tim nodded doubtfully. 'Is my dad going to be all right?'

'I hope so, Tim. He's very poorly just now, and we're doing everything we can to help him to get better. We'll tell you as soon as there's any more news, I promise.'

Tim was clearly still anxious, but he appeared to understand what Bryn was saying and he made no objection when Emily came and shepherded him away. Rhianna watched them go, and then turned to Bryn and said, 'What's been going on while I was on my break?'

'It looks as though the boy's father has been dabbling with cocaine. He collapsed and the boy called for help. It's a good job he did, because I don't think his dad would have made it otherwise. He was in a bad way when I first saw him—he was suffering from convulsions and then his heart went into tachyarrhythmia. After all that he arrested, and we had a struggle to get him back.'

'Do you think he's going to make it?'

'I don't know. It's touch and go at the moment.'

'That poor child.' Rhianna couldn't bear to think of what he was going through. It must be terrifying to see a parent collapse in front of you. 'I hope you manage to find his mother.'

'So do I.' Bryn's expression was grim. 'I can't believe the way that some people go on. Don't they have any thought for their children and what happens to them?'

'I expect they care, deep down, but in the end the addiction takes hold.' She was sad, reflecting on how some people ruined their lives without thinking. Wasn't this what Gwyneth was worried about? She knew that Colin couldn't be trusted, but that wouldn't stop him from trying to have access to Nathan once he discovered that he had a son.

'You're thinking about Colin, aren't you?' Bryn was watching her, carefully assessing her expression, and she was sure he must have noticed the downward turn of her mouth. 'He often used to end up in a bad way. I heard he had to be admitted to hospital at one time.'

'I can't help but think about him. He came near to losing his own life, and he threw away everything that went before. He had a good job and a woman who loved him, but it didn't make any difference in the end. The drugs would always win.'

'You did what you could for him, and I imagine Gwyneth did, too. You can't take on his troubles as well as your own. I should think you have enough on your plate, looking after Nathan.'

She nodded. 'That's true.' She gave a soft sigh, and then glanced at him, trying to read what was behind his eyes. For the most part, he kept his feelings hidden away, but he had been good to her, staying with her the other day when she was at a low ebb, and just now, when he had been talking to Tim, he had shown how kind and considerate he could be.

She said quietly, 'You were good with that boy,

Tim. He was upset and you managed to calm him down.' She made a faint smile. 'I thought you said you couldn't handle children.'

Bryn shrugged. 'I can't, generally, but it was easy to see what he was going through. It must be terrible to think that you're alone in the world, to feel helpless, and I wanted him to know that we would take care of him while he was here with us.'

'There's a limit to what we can do.'

'That's true, but I expect his mother will come back home before too long. She must have made arrangements to collect him from his father's flat.'

Rhianna nodded. 'Perhaps the boy should never have been allowed to stay with his father, given the circumstances.'

She watched Bryn closely, anxious to know what he thought about the situation. He might actually agree with her that there were no easy answers, and she might even be able to think again about letting him know the truth about Nathan. Her promise to Gwyneth was lying heavily on her.

'I think it would depend on what went on before and how the situation changes as time goes on. Some people are obviously hopeless cases, but I wouldn't say that was always the rule. Even addicts can get help and learn to behave in a different, more responsible way. As far as Tim's father is concerned, it's something that needs to be dealt with.'

'Do you think there is any hope for Colin?'

He was thoughtful for a moment. 'I think so. I saw

him the other day when he came in for his rehab session, and he seemed determined to go through with his programme. We spoke for a few minutes and it seemed to me that with the right help he could get through this.'

She lifted a brow. 'You spoke to him? I had the impression that you didn't want anything to do with him. When you first came here to work you saw him with me and thought he was up to no good, hanging around A and E. You didn't want him here.'

'That's true. Given that he's keeping up with his treatment, I decided that maybe I was being too harsh and that perhaps I should give him a second chance. We're all entitled to that, aren't we?'

'I suppose so.' There was no way she could tell him the truth about Nathan, she decided dejectedly. It was far too risky.

'Is something wrong?'

Her glance darted to him. 'Why do you say that?'

'You looked troubled for a moment. Are you finding things difficult? You've only just got over suffering from a virus, and I can imagine that it must be hard work looking after Nathan. Is there something I can do to help?'

She shook her head. 'There's nothing you can do, thanks all the same. I can manage.'

His mouth made a wry shape. 'I might have guessed that you would say that. It occurred to me that perhaps you need a break, a day out perhaps.

Would your father babysit for you so that you could get some time to yourself?'

'I wouldn't want him to do that. Nathan needs me. I'm out at work all day, and the time we have together is precious.'

He nodded. 'That's understandable.' He sent her a thoughtful glance. 'I'm free this weekend, and I could help out. The three of us could spend a day together…at the beach, maybe. Or even out in the countryside—whatever you like.'

She looked at him in surprise, her heart giving a little lurch. Could he really be saying that he wanted to spend time with her? 'Why would you want to do that? I thought you liked to be with your family at the weekends?'

'I do, but they're all away just now and, anyway, I could do with some practice in getting along with youngsters.'

She frowned. 'Why is that?' Any hope that she had that he might simply want to be with her was dashed. He had another reason for wanting to keep her company.

'I'm going to be attending a specialist course soon—it's to do with paediatric emergency measures mainly, and one of the sessions involves meeting a group of small children to see how they cope with visits to treatment centres. I think it might go better if I learn something about them before I go along on that. The age range is up to five years old and I don't really have a clue how I'm supposed to go on. I've lived a bachelor life for so long that infants are more or less an unknown quantity to me.'

She chuckled. 'Poor Bryn. I didn't think there was anything you couldn't do if you put your mind to it. I never imagined you'd be defeated by a bunch of four- and five-year-olds.'

His mouth indented. 'You might laugh, but I'm serious about this. What do you say? Do we have a date? We could go to the beach if it's fine, or if not, maybe a trip to the zoo?'

They both heard the sound of an ambulance siren in the distance, and Emily signalled to them that a couple of patients were being brought in. Rhianna nodded to show that they would be ready to receive them.

'Which do you think would be the best choice?' Bryn asked.

She thought about it for a moment, her mind half on the incoming patients. 'I think the zoo, probably. If it rains, there are always undercover attractions, and Nathan hasn't been to the zoo for a while.'

'Good. That's settled then. The zoo it is. I'll come and pick you both up on Saturday, if that's all right?'

'That's fine,' she said, moving towards the ambulance bay.

It was only later, when the rush had settled down, that she realised what she had committed herself to—a whole day spent with Bryn and Nathan. How on earth was she going to get through it without giving the game away that he wasn't her child? And how would she cope with having Bryn so near and yet so far away?

She had been confused and overwhelmed, having him in her kitchen the other day, so how would she manage the situation when they were out together, away from work? It didn't bear thinking about.

In the end, though, she reminded herself that this was only happening because of the course he was going to attend. He wasn't doing it out of any great desire to spend time with her.

On Saturday morning, Rhianna woke early and set about her arrangements, determined that she and Nathan would be ready when Bryn arrived, but things didn't go to plan.

She was sure that Nathan was looking forward to going to the zoo, but he was in a fractious mood from the moment he got out of bed, and she watched him in dismay as he found all sorts of reasons to delay getting ready.

'I don't want those,' he said crossly, tossing the navy trousers she had put out for him to wear to one side. 'I'm not wearing them.'

She inspected them closely. 'What's wrong with them?'

'They're scratchy and horrible,' he complained. 'I want my green ones. The ones that Mummy bought me for my birthday.'

'Mummy bought the navy ones as well,' Rhianna pointed out, using a patient tone. 'You've never minded them before.'

'Well, I do today. I want the green ones.' His chin went up in a gesture that reminded her so much of Gwyneth when she had been younger that she found herself relenting.

'You'll have to wait while I iron them, then,' she told him with a grimace. Arguing over a pair of trousers wasn't worth the hassle, but his recalcitrant attitude bothered her. What was she to do if he mentioned his mother while they were with Bryn? It didn't bear thinking about. One thing was for sure, though…this trip could turn out to be a nightmare one way or another.

'Eat your breakfast while I sort them out.'

'Don't want cereal,' he began. 'I want toast with jam, like Mummy makes. She always makes toast and jam when we go out.'

Rhianna frowned, trying to decipher his mutinous expression. She put down the trousers and laid an arm around his shoulders. 'You're missing her, aren't you? Are you worried that you might not see her today?'

'Will we see her?' He looked up at her, his grey eyes clouded.

'I'll take you to the hospital later on, after we've had tea. Would that be all right?'

He gave it some thought, then nodded. 'Why can't she come home?'

Rhianna's heart went out to him. He looked so small and vulnerable, standing there with a miserable droop to his mouth.

'She's still very poorly,' she explained. 'She wants to be at home with you, but she isn't strong enough to do that yet.'

'Can't the doctors make her better?'

'They're trying, but it took them a little while to find the right medicine for her, and being poorly has made her very tired.'

'Have they found the right medicine now?'

'I think so.' She had phoned the hospital earlier, and had spoken to the nurse in charge, but the report had been mixed. The antibiotics were beginning to work and bring the infection under control, but it had happened too late and there had been some worrying effects on Gwyneth's heart.

'We're concerned that one of her heart valves may have been damaged,' the nurse had said. 'She may need to have an operation to put things right.'

Looking at Nathan now, Gwyneth felt an overwhelming affection for him. If only she could protect him from everything that was going wrong. He was only four years old, and it was too soon for everything in his world to start falling apart.

'Tell you what,' she said, putting on a bright face, 'after we've been to the zoo, you could draw some pictures to show Mummy what it was like. I think she would like that, don't you?'

He nodded, and she was pleased to see that he was beginning to look a little more cheerful.

Bryn called for them a short time later. He was dressed in smart casual clothes again—dark green chinos and a matching shirt—and he looked so heart-meltingly attractive that her nervous system immediately shot into red alert.

'Who are you?' Nathan asked in a belligerent tone. He was casting suspicious looks at Bryn's chinos, as though he couldn't work out whether it was all right for the man to be wearing the same colour as him.

'I'm Bryn. I'm a friend of your mother,' Bryn answered with a smile.

Rhianna's heart missed a beat. Where was this conversation going to lead?

Nathan frowned. 'How do you know her?'

'I know her from a long time ago, when we used to live in the same village.'

'Oh.' Nathan seemed to accept that, and Rhianna let out a soft sigh of relief.

If the child asked any more questions like that, she would be a nervous wreck by the end of the day.

They piled into Bryn's car without too much fuss and arrived at the zoo some twenty minutes later.

Nathan was wide-eyed as he explored the various animal enclosures. Most of the camels were in their stalls, being fed, and as they walked past them Nathan said, 'Yuck. They stink.'

Bryn laughed. 'You're right. They do.' He seemed relaxed, as though he was enjoying the day, and Rhianna did her best to relax, too. It was a glorious summer day, with a clear blue sky overhead, and the sun was warm on her bare arms. She was wearing a sleeveless white top and a floaty cotton skirt in a soft, lightly patterned shade of yellow that reminded her of sunshine and flowers.

She walked side by side with Bryn as Nathan raced on ahead, stopping at each exhibit, but when they came to the gorilla enclosure, there was one part where they viewed the animal through a glass wall.

He was a huge beast, and he stared at them in return, one arm wound around the branch of a tree. A moment later he flung himself at the glass, as though he was heading straight for Rhianna.

'Oh!' Startled, she stumbled and almost fell backwards, but Bryn's arm came around her, holding her steady. Heat flooded through her.

'I wasn't expecting that,' she said breathlessly.

'It's a good thing the glass was reinforced,' he said with a chuckle. 'It makes you wonder, sometimes, who's watching who.'

Her heart was racing, but she wasn't sure whether it was from the shock of the animal flinging himself at her or whether it was because Bryn was still holding her. His long fingers cupped her shoulders, and she felt safe, protected, as though nothing in the world could harm her.

It was fanciful, of course. He had reacted instinctively, and it meant nothing. All the same, he kept his arm around her, and it seemed a natural thing to do. They walked around companionably, and the day seemed to be going well, but at lunchtime the tranquil atmosphere began to dissipate.

They went into the restaurant at the zoo, overlooking the flamingo pool, and Nathan was suddenly in an awkward mood once more. Rhianna had no idea what had brought it on.

'I don't want this,' he said looking down at his plate of food. He scowled at Bryn. 'I wanted chicken nuggets.'

Bryn lifted a brow. 'That's what I brought you,' he said in a mild tone.

Nathan pushed the plate away. 'No, you didn't. These are the wrong ones.'

'They might not be. You could try one, couldn't you? You might discover that you like them.'

'Don't want them,' Nathan persisted. 'They're the wrong shape.'

Rhianna bit her lip. It wasn't like Nathan to behave like this, and she couldn't fathom what was wrong with him. She glanced quickly at Bryn, disappointed that the day's pleasurable atmosphere was rapidly disintegrating.

She said, 'I'm sorry. He isn't normally this fractious. Perhaps he's tired. We've had a busy day up until now.'

'It's OK. If he doesn't want them, he doesn't. It's not worth making a fuss over.' He was being calm and easygoing about it, but all the same Rhianna felt uncomfortable.

They left the restaurant and wandered around some more. At one point, when it looked as though Nathan was tiring, Bryn offered to carry him, but Nathan resisted all his attempts to help him out.

'I'm not a baby,' the boy said scathingly.

'I know that,' Bryn murmured. 'I just that you might like a ride on my shoulders, that's all.'

Nathan frowned, thinking about it, and Rhianna wondered if he was regretting his display of annoyance, but pride won out and he set his jaw in a rebellious scowl and marched off in front of them.

Bryn sent her an oblique glance. 'I told you I don't have a knack with children,' he said with a wry smile.

'I don't think it's anything that you've done wrong,' Rhianna said, frowning. 'He started the day off badly, and things don't seem to be improving. I'm not quite sure what's the matter with him.'

Bryn shrugged. 'I'm a stranger to him, perhaps that's the reason.'

'Maybe,' she said, unconvinced. 'He can be a little shy sometimes.'

Things weren't any easier at the end of the afternoon when they were getting ready to leave the zoo. They stopped off at the souvenir shop, and Bryn bought Nathan a toy monkey that climbed a ladder and fell down the other side. Nathan appeared to be happy with it, and played quietly in the car on the way home, but just as they arrived back at the cottage he flung it to one side.

'Why did you do that?' Rhianna asked, getting out of the car and opening the door by his seat. She frowned, picking up the toy, and discovered that the wood was split in two. 'Look, the ladder's smashed now. Bryn bought this for you, and now you've broken it.'

'It was broked anyway,' he said defiantly, but she saw that he was looking a little shamefaced.

'Then you should have shown it to me, not thrown it down like that. That was naughty. I'm not very pleased with you, Nathan.'

The boy didn't answer, but stared sullenly out of the window. Rhianna's shoulders slumped in dismay.

She turned to Bryn, who was standing by her side. 'I'm sorry about this. Perhaps we'd better go inside the house.' Her eyes were troubled as she said haltingly, 'Would you like to come in for a coffee?'

He hesitated for a moment, and then shook his head. 'I'd better not. I should be getting back.' He gave her a quick smile, and added, 'Nathan's not in the best of moods, but he'll probably be more comfortable when I'm not around, and you'll have a better chance of settling him down. I'll see you at work on Monday.'

'All right.'

'It was a good day,' he said quietly, giving her a quick, searching look.

She nodded, but she knew that Nathan's irritability had cast a shadow over the afternoon. 'Yes, it was. Thanks for taking us.' She gave him a quick smile. 'And for putting up with the tantrums.'

His mouth indented a fraction, and he slid back into the driver's seat. She watched him drive away, and her heart was heavy with a sense of bitter disappointment.

What had she expected? The day had been good, better than she might have hoped for, but in the end it had all gone wrong and now she and Bryn were no closer than they had been before.

Perhaps she had been secretly wishing for much more than easygoing companionship, whereas he had simply wanted what he had said, to spend some time with her and Nathan to see if he could find the key to getting along better with youngsters.

In the house, she watched Nathan fling himself down on the settee. He looked grumpy and out of sorts, and that was pretty much the way that she felt, too.

'What was wrong with you today, Nathan?' she asked, going to sit down beside him. 'Didn't you enjoy seeing the animals? I thought that you would have a good time.'

He didn't answer, and she persisted, asking, 'Which animal did you like best of all?'

His shoulders hunched. 'I like the baby elephant,' he conceded after a while. 'Mummy says she likes the elephants best as well.'

'Does she?' Rhianna was quiet for a moment, thinking things through. 'Did Mummy take you to the zoo?' She hadn't thought of that until now. Was that what this rebellion was all about? Was he remembering when Gwyneth had taken him on an outing with her?

He nodded. 'We had dinosaur shapes for lunch and Mummy said they was yummy.'

'Oh, Nathan, come here.' Rhianna hugged him close to her. Suddenly, it all fell into place. No wonder he had been so difficult today, if he was missing his mother.

'I'm sorry that she couldn't go with us today,' she said quietly. 'We'll go and see her, though, and I'm sure she'd like to look at some pictures to remind her of what it was like when you went with her. Do you want to go and get your coloured pencils and some paper? You could make a start, if you like, while I get ready to take you to the hospital to see her.'

His face brightened, and he ran off to do as she had suggested.

Rhianna sat for a moment, thinking about everything that had happened. She couldn't explain any of this to Bryn, and that saddened her.

It made her even more unhappy to wonder what he might think of her if he ever found out the truth about her deception.

CHAPTER SIX

'I'M AFRAID she's taken a turn for the worse.'

Rhianna mulled over her phone conversation with the staff nurse on Gwyneth's ward as she headed towards the crèche with Nathan on Monday morning. Things were looking bad, and she didn't know what to do. She felt unbelievably helpless.

Suddenly, she became aware of Bryn walking in the direction of A and E. Nathan stopped in his tracks.

'We went to the zoo with you, didn't we?' he announced to Bryn, his face lighting up with recognition. 'I made some pictures of the animals for Mummy,' he confided, his voice lively with the memory. 'She liked them a lot. She said they was really good.'

Listening to him tell his tale to Bryn, Rhianna's heart lurched in sudden apprehension. What was he about to say?

'Did she? I'm glad about that,' Bryn said with a smile. He glanced at Rhianna, warmth kindling in his eyes before he turned back to the child. 'Did you enjoy our day out?'

Nathan nodded vigorously. 'It was funny when that g'rilla jumped at the window, wasn't it?' He grinned mischievously. 'That was really funny. We nearly felled over.'

'It was.' Bryn smiled in acknowledgement, but when he looked at Nathan again there was something odd about his expression, as though he was trying to puzzle something out, and Rhianna felt a sudden quiver of alarm.

Was Nathan about to alert him to the fact that she wasn't his mother? Panic made her pulse quicken, her heart beating so fast that tiny beads of perspiration began to break out on her brow.

The strain of keeping up this subterfuge was beginning to get to her, and it didn't help that she was already feeling anxious after the news about Gwyneth this morning.

Things were not going the way they should. She was worried about Gwyneth, and even more worried about how she could explain the latest setback to Nathan.

'We have to go,' she said apologetically. 'I'm running late again this morning and it takes time to get him settled at the crèche.' She started to usher Nathan away, throwing a backward glance at Bryn. 'I'll see you in A and E in a few minutes.'

'All right.' If he was surprised by her haste, he didn't show it, but he was still watching them as they started off along the corridor. He appeared to be deep in thought when he, too, eventually moved away.

Rhianna fretted inwardly, but resolutely turned Nathan towards the crèche. There was nothing she could do just now to get to the bottom of what Bryn might be thinking. Perhaps it was simply that he hadn't seen Nathan laugh like that before. In some ways he was a different boy from the one he had been on Saturday.

When she went to A and E a few minutes later, though, Bryn was busy with a patient, and when she glanced at him, he reacted in a perfectly normal manner, giving her a brief smile. Perhaps he had dismissed whatever thoughts had been going through his mind earlier. As the day wore on, Rhianna gradually felt her fears subside.

'We've a patient coming in by ambulance,' Bryn told her an hour or so later. 'He's been referred to us by his GP.'

'What's the problem?' Rhianna asked.

'A suspected kidney disorder. Apparently he's in pain, and he's been vomiting. According to the GP, he's also a little confused.'

Rhianna readied herself to receive the patient. The man was in his early fifties, and looked very pale and appeared to be suffering a considerable amount of pain.

'I've checked his notes on the computer,' Rhianna said. 'He's been showing signs of hypertension recently, and his blood pressure is still high now.'

She turned to her patient. 'Steven,' she said gently, 'we're going to look after you. Just try to relax as best you can, and we'll do our best to make you more comfortable. We need to do a few tests, just so that we can find out exactly what's wrong.'

Steven nodded, but she wasn't entirely sure that he had followed what she was saying, and as things progressed it was becoming clear that he was developing symptoms of kidney failure. She knew instinctively that Bryn was concerned about his condition, although he kept his thoughts to himself.

She had watched as he examined the man, and she was impressed by the lightness of his touch. When he had finished, he said, 'We need to assess the volume of urine, and test for infection.' He turned to Emily, who was assisting, and said, 'I need blood tests as well, urea and creatinine.'

Emily nodded. To Rhianna, he added in an undertone, 'We need to get things moving here. We had better do an ECG and obtain an urgent ultrasound scan. I'll organise pain relief for him.'

Rhianna had guessed a scan would be needed, and was already preparing the ultrasound. A few minutes later, as she passed the transducer over the region of the man's kidneys, she explained to him, 'This will give us a picture of your kidneys that we'll be able to see on the monitor. If there's any enlargement or blockage, it should show up on the screen.'

Bryn was watching the monitor closely. 'One of the kidneys is larger than the other,' he pointed out. 'I suspect that means that there's a narrowing of the artery somewhere. That could explain the hypertension.'

'He's very drowsy,' Rhianna pointed out after a while, in an aside to Bryn, 'and the volume of urine is falling. He's going into kidney failure.'

'All right. Get hold of the radiologist and let's get a renal arteriogram. That should show us if there's any blockage.'

The painkilling injection Bryn had given him was beginning to take effect, and Steven recovered for long enough for Rhianna to explain what they were planning to do.

'We're going to send you to Radiology,' she said quietly, 'so that we can investigate whether or not there's a blockage of some kind in one of your renal arteries. The radiologist will look after you. She'll inject a radiopaque substance into your arteries so that we can look at the blood supply to your kidneys. If she finds that there's a narrowing somewhere, she'll probably want to do what's called an angioplasty.'

'What's that?' Steven managed to ask.

'It's a technique that treats the narrowing of the blood vessel by introducing a balloon into the constricted area to widen it. She may need to use suction to remove any deposits blocking the arteries, but don't worry about the procedure. The radiologist will explain to you what she's going to do, and you'll be given a local anaesthetic so that you won't feel any pain.'

'Will that cure me?'

'Hopefully, it will, if the reason for your problems is found to be a narrowing of the artery. A lot of people find that their hypertension is brought under control after this procedure.'

He was obviously weak and in considerable discomfort, but he said unevenly, 'That's good. Thanks, Doctor.'

She smiled at him. He had behaved in such a stoical manner throughout his ordeal, and she very much hoped that he would come through this without any permanent damage to his system.

'You're welcome,' she said gently, momentarily laying a hand on his shoulder. 'I hope you'll soon be feeling better.'

She watched as he was wheeled down to Radiology a short time later, and her thoughts flitted to Gwyneth. She had heard last night that she, too, was suffering from problems with her kidneys because of her failing heart, and her doctors were doing what they could to stabilise her condition. If only she herself could be there with her, to be able to do something to help.

After Steven had been taken to Radiology, there was a lull in the department, and she was desperate for an opportunity to slip away and take a quick break. She needed a breath of fresh air, and there was a perfect place outside, a quiet area behind the building where she could escape for a minute or two and try to sort out the turmoil going round and round in her head.

Bryn was writing up his patient's notes as she hurried out there, and she didn't think he watched her leave.

It was tranquil out here, with an expanse of grass that was warmed by the sunshine, and there were trees that sheltered her from view. She leaned against the trunk of a silver birch and thought about Gwyneth and Nathan, and wondered how it was all going to turn out.

She wasn't alone for very long. Bryn approached just a few minutes later.

'I thought I might find you out here,' he said, coming to stand beside her. 'You look sad, as though you're deep in thought. Are you worried about the man we just sent to Radiology?'

She shook her head. 'No. I think he will come through this all right, but seeing him struggling with kidney failure like that made me think of Gwyneth and what she's going through.'

'Isn't she doing too well?'

She swallowed hard on a lump in her throat. 'Not really. She's been through a lot lately, and I don't think her problems can be remedied as easily as Steven's. They've managed to control the infection that was causing her so much trouble, but now it's left other things in its wake.'

'I heard that she was in a bad way,' he said, his tone sympathetic. 'I wanted to go and see her, but I'm not closely related, and the nurses wouldn't let me visit. They said that she was too ill to see anyone other than family. I'm sorry. It must be difficult for you.'

She nodded. 'I feel so helpless sometimes. As a

doctor, I think I should be able to do something for her, but instead I have to stand back and watch others do what they can. There's been one setback after another, and now with her kidneys not functioning as they should it's a worry. She looked so sick when I saw her last.'

'Is there anything that I can do to help?'

'No. I don't think so. She's getting specialist care, and I'm sure everyone's doing everything they can for her.'

It hurt her to think how desperately ill she was, and she couldn't bear to imagine how Nathan would feel if he learned how concerned they were about his mother's health. For the moment he was blissfully ignorant, the way only a four-year-old could be.

Her mouth trembled and she pressed her lips together so that Bryn wouldn't see her despair, but he was very perceptive.

'I'm here for you, Rhianna,' Bryn said now, reaching for her. 'You don't have to bear this alone, you know. Lean on me, and I'll do whatever I can to help you to get through this.' His arms enclosed her, and it felt so good, so soothing and natural to have him hold her this way, that she didn't even think of resisting. She felt secure in his embrace, safe, as though all her troubles might melt away if only she could stay here, like this, locked in his arms.

He drew her head down towards him, and she rested her cheek against his chest, calmed by the steady beating of his heart. When his long fingers gently stroked her auburn curls, she felt cherished, comforted, in a way that she hadn't experienced since her childhood.

'I'm sorry to fall apart like this,' she mumbled after a while, looking up at him. 'I don't know what came over me. I'm so used to managing things. It isn't like me to give in. I'll be fine now, really.'

He shook his head. 'You have a lot on your plate, with one thing and another. First your father's heart attack, and the worries that followed on from that, then Gwyneth falling ill, and through it all you have to cope with looking after Nathan. You mustn't worry about letting your feelings out. It can't be doing you any good to keep things bottled up.'

He brushed his thumb gently over her trembling lower lip, tracing its soft curve. 'Besides, you and I go back a long way, and there's no shame in sharing things with me. I'm glad to be here for you in any way I can. I want you to know that.'

'You're being so good to me,' she said huskily, giving him a tremulous smile. 'Thank you for that.'

His gaze travelled over her, assessing her features with slow deliberation, shifting from the troubled crease of her brow, across the sweeping lines of her cheekbones and down to the soft fullness of her mouth.

'Let me help,' he murmured. 'Let me do what I can to take your troubles away.' Slowly, he bent his head, and feathered her lips with his own. 'I hate to see you hurting,' he said huskily, and then he lightly claimed her mouth once more.

The kiss was unexpected, gentle and explorative, and it took her breath away, making her senses soar in spellbound fulfilment. This was what she had longed for, what she had dreamed of for so many years, and now it felt perfect, so beautifully right that this was happening. She wanted to savour it for ever.

The moment didn't last, though. The sound of an ambulance siren brought them both back with crashing force to the present and the reality of their surroundings.

She was dizzy for a second or two, her head reeling with the wonder of what had just taken place.

But it should never have happened, should it? What if somebody had come along and discovered them? Dazed, she looked at him, wondering how on earth she would have explained herself.

Bryn drew in a deep breath and held her away from him at arm's length, as though he was reluctant to let her go. He steadied her, and it was just as well because she was still light-headed from the sensation of his mouth on hers. Her lips tingled as the memory of that kiss stayed with her.

They heard a vehicle pull up in the ambulance bay, the siren still sounding in the background, and for a moment it was lost in the confusion of the alarm bells going off in her head.

'Bryn…I…I don't know…' She stared at him, her

heart pounding, her mind racing, trying to make sense of what had just happened.

'I know. I'm sorry. I don't know what I was thinking,' he said. 'Let's try to forget that it happened, shall we?'

Forget it? Her eyes widened in shock as though he had slapped her. How could she ever forget that kiss?

He didn't seem to share her difficulty. 'I should get back to work,' he said, his tone matter-of-fact. 'You stay here for a while and get yourself together. You're due a break anyway, and I can deal with whatever's coming in. I'll call for you if I need you.'

He paused. 'Just remember that if I can do anything at all, help in any way, you only need to ask.'

'I will.'

He gave her a brief smile and walked away from her, and Rhianna pulled in a shaky breath. He was so calm, so regretful...and now he was putting it behind him.

He thought of her as a friend, nothing more, and the kiss had simply been his way of saying that she wasn't on her own through any of this. That was the truth of it, wasn't it? Much as she might have hoped for something more than that, it wasn't going to happen, was it?

The knowledge of that left her feeling bewildered and dismayed. How was she going to go on working with him, knowing that every time she saw him she would remember the thrill of being in his arms?

When she finally went back to the treatment room, though, Bryn was no longer there.

'He was called out to a road traffic accident where there was a cardiac emergency,' Emily told her. 'He went out with the paramedics to assist.'

He did that sometimes, she recalled, and perhaps it was just as well that she didn't have to face him again right now. She didn't know how she would cope with having him so near and yet so far away.

He hadn't returned by lunchtime, and she went to see Nathan for a while and then wandered down to the hospital restaurant to grab a bite to eat. Nathan was sharing a special picnic lunch with the staff and children at the crèche, and she left him enjoying the novelty of it.

She had just fetched herself a tray of food, which she planned to eat outside, when Colin appeared in the corridor and came and walked alongside her.

'I was just taking my lunch out to the quadrangle,' she said.

'We must have had the same idea,' he murmured. 'Would you mind if I join you? I was going to take my lunch there, too, and sit on a bench to eat it. Could we sit and talk for a while, do you think?'

She looked at him and saw that he was carrying a pack of sandwiches and a polystyrene cup.

'Of course,' she said lightly. She would have preferred to sit alone for a while with her thoughts, but she had promised him her support and it would have been churlish to refuse.

They found a seat in a quiet part of the hospital's landscaped gardens. There were several people passing by on their way to the various departments of the hospital, but it didn't detract from the peacefulness of the scene. There were flowering shrubs a few yards from where they sat in the courtyard, and they were shaded from the brilliant rays of the sun by trees whose branches swayed lightly in the faint breeze.

Rhianna ate her baked potato and toyed with the melted cheese on her fork as she listened to Colin explain about his rehabilitation.

'It has been hard to get through things sometimes,' he confessed. 'There are times when I come close to slipping, when I want to put everything out of my mind and take a quick fix to blot things out, but I know that people will check up on me, and it helps to keep me in line. I'm afraid of letting them down, and of letting myself down, too.'

'It was never going to be easy, was it?' she said softly. 'Have you managed to find work yet?'

He shook his head. 'I've been for one or two interviews, but no one's offered me a position up to now. I think they feel that I'm not far enough along in the programme for me to be committed to seeing it through to the end.'

'So you have time on your hands?'

He nodded. 'That's the worst thing, really. It gives me too much time to think about the way things are going.'

'Could you try to learn a new skill—join some

classes, perhaps? There must be something out there for you to try, and you might find that your mentor could help get you enrolled. You used to be good at engineering design work, didn't you? Maybe you could take a refresher course?'

'I hadn't thought of that.' His eyes lit up a fraction. 'I could make some enquiries, couldn't I? Find out what the possibilities are.' His mouth curved in a smile, and he reached over and gave her a hug. 'Thanks, Rhianna. You're good to me. I can always rely on you to come up with something.'

She smiled in return, looking up at him with caution in her glance. 'It may not be easy to get exactly what you want, but you could think through your options, couldn't you?'

'Bless you. I'll give it a whirl. I've an appointment with my adviser tomorrow. I'll have a word with him about it.' He hugged her once more.

'Let me know how you get on,' she said, and he nodded.

Rhianna glanced at the watch on her wrist. 'I have to go back to work, but I expect I'll see you again before long. Take care, won't you?'

'I will.' He was thoughtful for a moment, as though he was working through something that troubled him. He said at last, 'Maybe when I've sorted myself out, I'll go and see Gwyneth and find out how she's getting along. It's been a long while since we were in touch, and she might have got over our differences by now.'

Rhianna gave him a quick, cautious glance. 'I don't think that would be a good idea just yet.'

'You don't?' Perhaps her anxiety showed, because he looked as though she had dealt him a blow. 'I don't want to upset her, but I know things were bad between us before I left and I was hoping I could start to put things right. I can understand if she doesn't want to see me.'

'I'm sure there'll come a time when you can both sort things out, but she hasn't been well, and she can't take any upset just now.' She bit her lip, wondering if she had said too much.

Colin was frowning. 'I'm sorry. I'd heard rumours, but no one is telling me very much. How long do you think it will be before she's well again?'

'I don't know. Leave it for a while, and concentrate on your own recovery.'

'OK,' he said cautiously, 'if you think that's the best thing to do. '

He looked as though he was full of doubts, but he wasn't pushing it, and from his expression Rhianna guessed that he thought she was simply making excuses to keep him away. She made an effort to smooth things over.

'It's just that this is a particularly bad time for her right now. Perhaps in a few months she'll be stronger and more able to cope.'

He nodded, but still appeared to be unconvinced, and Rhianna went back to work with her mind racing.

Bryn was back in the department, sitting at the

desk, reading through a patient's file, and he looked up at her as she walked into the room. His glance was guarded and assessing as he watched her approach, and she wondered what was wrong.

Perhaps he was recalling their closeness from earlier in the day and was still regretting it.

She decided to pretend that she was unconcerned. 'How's it going?' she asked him lightly. 'I heard that you went out on an emergency call. Did it turn out all right?'

'Not exactly,' he said. He pushed the file back into the wire tray. 'My patient's in Intensive Care right now.'

She frowned. 'I'm sorry.'

'So am I.' He searched her features. 'When I came back to the hospital, I saw you sitting outside with Colin.'

'Oh, did you?' She winced inwardly. There was no privacy at all in this place. 'We had lunch together.'

'Yes, I know. He's still very fond of you, isn't he? You seemed to be getting along very well with each other.'

'I suppose he is fond of me. We've always got on fairly well together.' She made a vague, dispassionate gesture. 'I've told you before, I want to do what I can to help him get his life back together again.'

He nodded. 'I know that's important to you.' He looked at her steadily, and his eyes were so intensely blue at that moment that she felt as though he was trying to see into her very soul.

He said slowly, 'He's Nathan's father, isn't he?'

Her mouth dropped open. How on earth had he found that out? Quickly, she tried to recover herself and said, 'What makes you think that? You never mentioned it before.'

'It didn't occur to me until today. When I came across you and Nathan this morning, I knew there was something that I wasn't sure about, but just now, seeing you with Colin made me realise what it was I was missing. The likeness is there, in the way they both tilt their heads to one side and smile. There's an odd little quirk about their mouths, and the similarity in their expressions struck me as soon as I saw Colin today. They have more or less the same hair colour and the same eyes.' He shook his head. 'Nathan's hair even has a faint curl in it, like Colin's. I can't believe that I missed it before.'

Rhianna stared at him, transfixed. Could she deny it? Wouldn't that just make matters ten times worse than they were already?

She said, 'No one can be that certain of a likeness, surely?'

'I can,' he said. 'There's no doubt in my mind at all.' His eyes pinioned her. 'Why didn't you tell me?'

Her mouth made an odd quiver. She could tell from his expression that he wasn't going to be swayed now that he had reached his own conclusions.

'What would have been the point in telling you? He doesn't know about Nathan. I want to keep it that way.'

His mouth made a cynical twist. 'No wonder things went wrong between you and Gwyneth for a while. She must have been doubly hurt. Colin let her down in many ways, and you of all people betrayed her by having a relationship with him.'

'You don't know how things are,' she managed. 'You can't possibly understand.'

'You're right.' His mouth made a hard line. 'I don't.'

'Gwyneth was upset with me because I tried to warn her about Colin's drug habit. She didn't believe me. She thought I was trying to stop her from marrying him.'

'Exactly. You *were* trying to stop her.'

'Yes, but not because I wanted him for myself.'

'I don't believe you. And, anyway, you not only dated him before he married Gwyneth, but it's plain to see that you dated him afterwards.'

'It isn't true, Bryn. You have it all wrong.'

Emily came over to the desk just then and said quietly, 'There's been another major road traffic accident. We have four casualties on their way in.'

He stood up. 'OK, let's get ready for them.' He moved away without a backward glance, and Rhianna's shoulders drooped in defeat.

She was done for. Any chance she might have had of winning Bryn's trust and love was gone for ever now. He had never had time for Colin, and if he believed that he had fathered her child, he would turn his back on her and lose any respect for her that he had ever had.

He had always been fond of Gwyneth, and he had stood by her, sharing her pain at the break up of her marriage, and he simply wouldn't understand how Rhianna could have let this happen.

The irony of it was that she wanted Gwyneth's happiness more than anyone, and her loyalty to her cousin had lost her any hope of ever being close to Bryn again.

A siren sounded in the distance, and she straightened up and readied herself to go and meet the ambulance. There was work to be done, and maybe, if she filled her hours by keeping busy, that would serve to take away some of her pain.

CHAPTER SEVEN

'WE'RE losing her airway,' Bryn said on a warning note. 'I'm going to try to buy some time by giving her nebulised adrenaline and saline, but you had better get hold of the anaesthetist. He may need to do an emergency intubation.'

'I'll give him a call.' Rhianna had watched in alarm as the three-year-old child they were treating suddenly slumped, but now she hurried away to phone for help and arranged for the ear, nose and throat specialist to come down at the same time.

'What's happening to my little girl? Why isn't she talking any more?' The child's mother had been watching proceedings and now her voice rose in panic. 'Why isn't she breathing? Please, tell me what's happening. What are you doing?'

'Sarah's throat is swelling inside because of the infection, and it's making it difficult for her to breathe,' Rhianna explained, as she came back to the group assembled around the child's bedside.

They hadn't been able to intubate from the outset because of the swollen tissues and the risk of making matters worse, and it was a disturbing situation for everyone.

Rhianna was trying her best to keep her voice calm

as she spoke to the mother, but inside she was desperately worried for the little girl. She had gone downhill so fast that they were all concerned for her safety.

By now, Bryn must have decided that they couldn't wait any longer because she saw that he was preparing to do an urgent cricothyroidotomy.

'We've been giving her oxygen through the face mask up to now,' she told the mother, 'but it isn't helping her at the moment, and Dr Bryce is going to make an incision so that we can put a tube in to help her to breathe.'

Sarah's mother began to weep noisily. 'But she's so tiny. This can't be happening. I can't bear it.'

Rhianna could understand her anxiety, but her presence in the treatment room was slowing them down, and she was worried that her agonised cries might have an adverse effect on the child. The little girl needed to stay calm and be reassured, and this wasn't helping.

'I think perhaps it would be better if you leave us to work with her for a little while,' she said as gently as she could. She signalled to Emily. 'Our nurse will take you to a room where you can wait for a while, and she'll try to explain to you what's happening. As soon as we can, I promise you we'll bring you back to be with Sarah.'

It was a distressing time for all of them. The little girl had been brought in suffering from an infection of the epiglottis, and her condition had rapidly deteriorated. They were all desperate to do what they could for her.

Emily ushered the tearful woman away and Rhianna went back to helping Bryn. The anaesthetist arrived in double quick time to stand by for emergency intubation, but Bryn had already pierced the child's cricothyroid membrane. A withdrawal of air confirmed that he had made the incision correctly, and then he slid the cannula over the needle and used a Y-connector to hook up with the oxygen supply.

The girl's colour began to improve, and Rhianna gave a faint sigh of relief. She prepared to give the child antibiotics to combat the infection, and guessed that things would look up for the little girl from here on, but the episode was still bothering her a while later.

'That was a close call,' she murmured, watching Bryn as he examined Sarah once more. 'Much too close for comfort. I thought this kind of infection was less likely to happen these days.'

'It is.' Bryn's tone was brisk. 'Since the Hib vaccine was introduced we've seen less and less of it, but it may be that she hasn't had the full course of vaccinations yet, or there may be some other cause. It's unfortunate, but this kind of infection still happens sometimes.'

'You kept a clear head through it all,' she said as they moved away from the girl's bedside and left the child in the care of a nurse. 'I think I might have gone to pieces if I had been the one in charge of her.'

'No, you wouldn't. You'd have acted instinctively, and you would have done whatever had been necessary.'

He glanced at her obliquely. 'I've seen you deal with stressful situations before, remember? Even when your father had his heart attack, you were on your knees trying to help him. Before I came into the pharmacy and saw what was happening, you had already given him aspirin and put him in a position that made him more comfortable and able to cope. At that time you had no medical training whatsoever.'

'You don't know how relieved I was that you came along and knew what you were doing.'

He made a grimace. 'We do what we have to when we're driven. All the more so when children are involved.'

'Maybe you're right,' she acknowledged. She sent him a cautious look from under her lashes. At least he was talking to her now in a reasonably friendly fashion. After what had happened the other day, when he had realised that Nathan was Colin's son, he had hardly passed the time of day with her. She had been afraid that things would never be the same between the two of them again.

'I am.' He threw her a sharp glance. 'Perhaps you should bring Sarah's mother back into the room now. She must be overwrought, not knowing what's happening to her child.'

Rhianna's face paled. 'Do you think I was wrong in sending her out?'

'I didn't say that, but I can imagine that it must be traumatising to see your child suffer and not be able to do anything to help. Thankfully, I've never been faced with that situation.'

'I'll go and fetch her.' Her tone was subdued. She glanced at him again, surreptitiously, but he was frowning, deep in thought. A moment later he went in search of his next patient.

Rhianna hurried to the waiting room and explained to Sarah's mother that the child was out of any immediate danger and that she could go and sit with her.

'We'll be admitting her so that we can bring the infection under control,' she told her. 'I'm sorry that I had to ask you to leave. It must have been difficult for you, but we needed to keep her calm and we had to be able to concentrate on making sure that she could breathe.'

'Is she going to be all right?'

'I think so. Once the antibiotics start to do their job, things should improve fairly rapidly.'

'Good. Will I be able to stay with her if she's being admitted?'

'Yes, we'll make arrangements for you to be with her.'

'Thank you.'

Rhianna left her with the little girl, and went back to work. Bryn was nowhere to be seen, and she guessed that he was busy with a patient.

It seemed that things were still not going to get any

better between the two of them. Her sense of hope had been short-lived.

By the end of the week, she had other things on her mind. Gwyneth was to undergo surgery for a damaged heart valve, and that made Rhianna even more concerned about the future.

'You will take care of Nathan if anything should happen to me, won't you?' Gwyneth asked in a pleading note. 'I know he'll be all right with you. You're good for him.'

Gwyneth was trying hard to cope with her illness, but it was all getting too much for her. Rhianna could see that from the way she sank back against her pillows and briefly closed her eyes, as though she was summoning up strength from deep within her.

'You're going to get well and take care of him yourself,' she said firmly. 'Don't you dare give up on me. Nathan needs you. We both need you back home with us, and Dad says you're to do as you're told, take your medicine and come home because the place is empty without you. Enough of lying here in bed and taking life easy.' She smiled, and Gwyneth tried to respond with a brief tilt of her own mouth.

'You're both terrible bullies,' she said weakly.

'You can do it,' Rhianna told her. 'Once you've had this operation, you'll feel as though you're a new woman. Things won't seem nearly so hard to cope with, believe me.'

'I know,' Gwyneth said tiredly. 'I know…but you must take care of Nathan for me. I'm relying on you.'

'And he's relying on you.'

Gwyneth closed her eyes and drifted into sleep, and Rhianna watched her for a minute or two, praying that she wouldn't give in. She had to get well, for Nathan's sake.

There was another shock waiting for Rhianna when she returned to A and E that afternoon.

Bryn met her at the desk and said quietly, 'The police have been here, trying to get in touch with you.'

Rhianna felt the colour drain from her face. 'What did they want? Is it Nathan—has something happened to him?'

'I don't think it was anything like that,' Bryn said in a reassuring tone, seeing her panicked expression. 'They wouldn't say why they needed to see you, but I'm sure they would have told me if it was something to do with Nathan.'

She was still distressed that they had come here looking for her, and couldn't get the thought that it might be something to do with the boy out of her mind. 'He was fine this morning. He was bubbly and cheerful, full of what he was going to do today,' she said faintly. 'Are you certain it wasn't anything to do with him? Why else would they want to talk to me?'

'Come and sit down,' Bryn ordered, taking her by the arm and leading her towards the doctors' lounge. 'I didn't mean to upset you. I'm sure it can't be anything to be concerned about, or they would have left a message of some sort.'

'My father, then?' she asked unhappily. 'Do you think it might be something to do with him? I spoke to him last night and he was perfectly all right.'

He gently pressured her into a seat by the table. 'I've told you, I'm sure they would have said right away if it was something like that. Why don't you phone him and speak to him if you're concerned, and go up to the crèche and check on Nathan if it will put your mind at rest? When you've done that, you can ring the police and find out what the problem is. The officer left a contact number.'

'I'll give him a call, then.' She looked up at Bryn, still feeling shaky. 'I'm sorry, I wasn't expecting this. It took me by surprise. I'll be all right in a minute or two.'

He reached for a coffee-cup and filled it from the jug. He added cream and sugar and then passed the cup to her, saying, 'Drink this and get your thoughts together. Do you want to go up to the crèche first of all? It won't take more than a few minutes to reassure yourself that all's well, but I'm sure they would have rung here if anything was wrong. The same with your father. His assistant would have contacted you by now.'

'You're right, of course.' She sipped at the hot coffee, and waited for it to warm her. 'They have my mobile number as well as my work phone number and my bleeper. I'm worrying unnecessarily.'

She took another sip of her drink and added, 'Nathan isn't at the crèche any more. When the summer holidays finished last week, he went back to nursery school, but they know how to get in touch with me.'

'Then all you have to do is ring the police number and find out what it's all about. Shall I stay with you while you do that? I don't want you to suffer any more shocks, and if there's anything I can do, you only have to ask.'

'Thanks.' She looked up at him and gave him a grateful smile. 'I'd like it if you would stay.' Bit by bit, she was beginning to calm down. He made her feel safe just by standing there, as though he was the one unyielding force in her life. He was strong, mentally and physically, and she felt that she could cope with anything as long as he was there by her side.

There was a telephone on the table, and he pushed it towards her. 'Go ahead and dial. Get it over with, and you'll know what it is that you have to deal with.'

She did as he suggested, and when she spoke to the police officer she was taken aback to discover that this was all about Colin.

'He hasn't turned up for his rehabilitation sessions for a while,' the officer told her. 'His doctor and his welfare officer asked us if we could find out what had happened to him. They've tried his flat, but he wasn't there, and the neighbours haven't seen him either. He gave your name as someone who could be contacted in case of emergency, and we wondered if you know anything of his whereabouts?'

'I'm afraid I don't,' she said, puzzled about what could have happened to him. 'I haven't seen him for more than a week. I thought perhaps he had gone away for a few days.'

She put the receiver down and tried to think things through. The last time she had seen Colin he had been troubled because she had asked him not to get in touch with Gwyneth. By doing that, had she inadvertently pushed him into a relapse? It wouldn't have been the first time that he had fallen by the wayside.

It was disheartening, though, because she thought he had been doing so well.

'Do you want to tell me about it?' Bryn asked.

'I'm afraid I overreacted,' she said, feeling a little foolish, now. 'It wasn't anything at all to do with Nathan or my father. They're looking for Colin.' She took another sip of her coffee. 'Apparently, he hasn't turned up for the last few rehab sessions with his doctor, and they think something might have happened to him.'

Bryn's expression was grim. 'Do you think he might have got back in with his old crowd?'

'I don't know. I don't think so, because the welfare officer checked up on that and didn't come up with anything. I'm not sure what can have happened to him. I suppose he might have gone to the coast for a while to think things through.' It made her sad to think that he might have thrown away everything they were trying to do to get his life back together again.

'You look unhappy,' Bryn said. 'Were you hoping that he might have sorted himself out? I imagine you want to build some kind of life with him, for Nathan's sake. The boy must be coming up to an age where he wants to know about his father.'

Rhianna pulled in a shaky breath. 'So far, Nathan hasn't asked too many questions about his background,' she said truthfully. 'There are so many single-parent families these days that I suppose he doesn't stand out too much among his friends. It's the way things are.'

'But it doesn't have to be that way for always, does it? There will come a time when Colin will have to be told that he has a son. He has a right to know about him, and Nathan has a right to know about his dad.'

'That isn't going to happen. Not yet, anyway. Colin needs to be completely clear of his drug habit before he can have anything to do with his child. It wouldn't be safe for him to have free access otherwise.'

'But that's what you're hoping for?'

'It would be a good thing, wouldn't it, if only he was the person he should have been when he was a young man. He had a lot of potential, but it was all wasted.'

Bryn's eyes narrowed on her. 'I thought you felt that he was responding to rehabilitation?'

'I thought he was, yes, but I can't be sure, especially now that he's gone missing.'

'I'm sorry,' Bryn said. There was something in his tone that made her glance at him searchingly, something cold and remote, but his thoughts were closed to her, as though he had shut himself off from her and had made up his mind that he wasn't going to allow her in.

She was hurt that he was distancing himself from her, but there was nothing she could do to put things right. 'It isn't your problem,' she said. 'You've been there for me today, and I'm glad of that. It meant a lot to me.'

'Have you any thoughts about what you might do?'

'Right now?' She shook her head. 'I might go and look for him…make some enquiries at the places where he might have gone. I know he liked to spend time at a little cottage by the sea when he was younger. It used to belong to his grandfather. If it was vacant, he might have booked himself in there for a day or so.'

'The holiday season's over, so there's a good chance it might have been available. Why don't you go over there now and see for yourself?'

She looked up at him, startled by the suggestion. 'I have to work…'

'You'll not be fit for much more today, given the state you were in earlier. Perhaps, with Gwyneth being ill, too, this has all been too much for you. I think you should take the rest of the afternoon off.' His tone was very matter-of-fact, as though there was no discussion to be had.

'I have to fetch Nathan from nursery school in a while.'

'There's still time for you to do both things. I know

the cottage you mean, and it isn't far away. Go and see if Colin is there.'

'All right.' She wasn't going to argue with him. He was being cool and calm and allowing her to deal with the situation the best way she could, and if it broke her heart that he was so withdrawn from her, there was nothing she could do to put that right just now.

She found the cottage some twenty minutes later, an isolated building set back from the shingle beach by a low cliff that was washed by the incoming tide. Trees surrounded the house, their branches overhanging the walls and providing seclusion from prying eyes.

Rhianna walked up the path and knocked on the front door, but there was no answer. She wandered around the outside of the cottage, peering in through the windows as she went, hoping for some clue as to the occupant, but without any luck.

Then she came to the back of the building and saw that a car was parked in a standing area that had once been part of a garden and now opened out onto a dirt track that led to the coast road some distance away.

Inspecting it closely, she noticed that there was an envelope on the dashboard, and she was able to make out part of the address. She recognised Colin's name, and a feeling of relief flooded through her. She had found him.

Going around to the back of the house, she knocked on the door and called his name. There was no answer, and after a moment's hesitation she tried the doorhandle and realised that it was unlocked.

'Colin, are you there?'

A muffled sound came from upstairs, and she called again, 'It's Rhianna. I'm coming upstairs.'

A moment later, she was shocked to find that Colin was lying on the floor of the main bedroom, a trickle of dried blood on the carpet coming from a wound at his temple.

'Colin—what happened?' She dropped to her knees beside him. 'Can you talk?'

Sick at heart, it crossed her mind that he might have taken something that had caused him to be in this state, but when he managed to mouth a few words, she realised that this was not the case.

She laid the back of her hand on his forehead and realised that he was burning up with fever. She wondered how long he had been in this state.

'You're ill, aren't you?' she said, the impact of what must have happened to him hitting her as she saw the stain of blood on the dresser, where he must have fallen and banged his head. 'You fell because you're feverish and you were unsteady on your feet.'

He tried to move his arm, but she said, 'No, don't try to move. I'll go and get help.'

She rang for the ambulance, and then, in desperation, called Bryn. 'I've found Colin. I think he has a virus of some sort,' she told him in a breathless rush, 'and he's fallen and banged his head. He must have knocked himself out for a while.'

'Slow down,' Bryn said. 'Take your time and focus on what has to be done.'

'I will. But I'm worried about Nathan,' she said, taking a breath and going on more slowly. 'He's due to be collected from nursery school any time now, and I don't have their number to ring them. It's the Early Days nursery, and I wondered if you could look them up for me so that I can let them know what's happened? It will be at least a half an hour before I can get there to pick Nathan up.'

'Leave it with me. I'm about to go off duty now, and I'll pick him up for you. I'll get the nursery to give you a ring to confirm that it's all right for me to collect him in your place.'

Relief swamped her. 'Thanks, Bryn. I owe you.'

'You're welcome. I don't know how long you're going to be,' he added, 'so I'll take him to the soft-play centre at the pub near your house. He can jump about in the ball park for a while and lose his energy on the rope ladders and so on.'

'That sounds like a good idea.' She was filled with relief that he was doing this for her.

The ambulance came within a few minutes and the paramedics made sure that Colin was lifted safely on board.

'You'll be all right now, Colin,' Rhianna reassured him. 'You'll be admitted to hospital and the doctors will give you something to bring your fever down. You've a nasty head wound, but it doesn't appear to have knocked you out for long, and I think you'll be on the mend soon.'

He tried to thank her, but she squeezed his hand gently and said softly, 'I'll give the hospital a call later to see how you're doing, and I'll come and see you tomorrow. Just try to relax and I'm sure you'll be feeling more like your old self soon.'

She stood and watched as the ambulance pulled away a few minutes later, and then she locked up the cottage and went back to her car. Nathan would be waiting for her, and she didn't want him to be fretting unduly.

As things turned out, he was more than happy to be with Bryn. 'I've been swinging on the ropes and going through the tunnels,' he told her excitedly. Then with a frown, he added, 'I made you a picture at school, but I had it in my pocket and it fell out and it got squidged.'

He handed her a mangled crayon drawing and she enthused over it with a show of delight.

'I lost my sock as well,' he said. He pulled a face. 'Don't know where it is.'

She ruffled his hair. 'We won't worry about that. There are plenty more socks at home.'

She looked up at Bryn and said quickly, 'Thanks for fetching him for me. I was so worried when I knew that I was going to be late. Did you have any problems? You obviously managed to find the place all right.'

'No problems,' he said. He glanced at his watch. 'I have to go. I promised my brother and his wife that I would go over to their place for dinner, and there are things I need to do first.'

He seemed a little abrupt, and Rhianna was disturbed by the cool set of his mouth. When she thought about it, dinner seemed to be a long way off, unless his brother had an early schedule. Was Bryn simply making an excuse to leave her?

'You seem to have coped well with looking after Nathan,' she murmured, playing for time in the hope of discovering what was wrong. Nathan had taken himself back into the ball park. 'He's taken to you, even though you say you aren't good with children. You've certainly found the key to managing him.'

'That's because he's an easy child to get along with.' His jaw flexed almost imperceptibly, but Rhianna caught the movement and wondered what was bothering him.

'Did he give you any trouble at all?'

'None. He's a delightful child.'

'But something's wrong. I know it is. I can sense it.' She searched his face. 'What is it?'

'The nursery staff were very accommodating. They told me that you were never late in picking him up, even though you had to juggle your work and the problems of coping with a small child. They said it was amazing how well you coped with looking after him while his mother was in hospital.'

He looked at her directly, his blue eyes as cold as

glass. 'Of course, I didn't tell them that I had no idea what they were talking about, since I had been led to believe that you were his mother. It would have put me in a very awkward position, don't you think?'

She was aghast. It hadn't occurred to her in the anxiety about getting Colin to hospital that he might discover the truth of the situation.

'I'm sorry,' she said. 'I'm really sorry you had to find out that way.' Her mouth was suddenly as dry as dust. 'I can explain everything.'

'It's too late for that now,' he said briskly. 'You had every opportunity to tell me what was going on before this. You didn't take it. Instead, you chose to lie to me at every turn.'

'I didn't want to.'

'But you did. For some reason of your own, you preferred deception to the truth.' His expression was wintry. 'I'm leaving now. I hope Nathan at least understands what's going on in his life.'

She called out to him as he turned away, but he didn't come back to her.

He strode out to the car park and climbed into his car. He drove off without hesitation, while she stood there by the door of the play centre, wishing that things could have been different. He would never forgive her.

CHAPTER EIGHT

'How is Gwyneth?' Rhianna asked the nurse on duty on her cousin's ward. 'Did the operation to replace her heart valve go well?'

The nurse appeared hesitant. 'Everything went more or less to plan,' she told her, 'but there were some setbacks while she was under the anaesthetic, and they didn't help. She was very weak after the surgery, and we're quite worried about her. She's been through a lot lately.'

Rhianna absorbed the information despondently. 'It's been a worrying time for all of us,' she said in a quiet voice. 'I've been waiting and hoping for her to get through this and to come out of it stronger than before.'

'It's going to be some time before we can say that she's out of the woods for certain. At least the medication has put an end to the infection that was raging through her body, and we just have to hope that she'll be strong enough to keep going.'

In a brighter tone, the nurse added, 'She's a fighter, though. I'm sure that will stand her in good stead. Through it all, she's kept her little boy at the forefront of her mind.'

'That works both ways. Nathan is constantly talking about her, too.' Rhianna's thoughts swung to the way Nathan had badgered her yesterday to let him see his mother. He was impatient for her to be well again and he didn't really understand that it would take time for her to get over her operation. He fully expected it to be an instant cure. He wasn't letting up, and it hurt to have to tell him that they must wait a little while longer.

'When do you think she'll be able to see visitors?' she asked now.

'Later on today perhaps, but only for a few minutes and we'll be strictly limiting the number of people who can see her. You should give it at least another day or so before you can expect any real change in her condition,' the nurse advised. 'We should be able to tell you more then.'

'Thank you.'

Rhianna made her way back to A and E. She was more anxious than ever about Gwyneth's failing health and what she really needed right now was time to calm herself down and rid herself of her worries, but there was no way that would be possible here.

The pace was unrelenting, with an influx of accident patients and cardiac emergencies, along with two people who had been brought into the department suffering from what turned out to be strokes.

'We have to refer this man to the stroke unit as quickly as possible,' Bryn said, pushing the patient's notes back into the tray on the desk. 'Give the unit a call and get things moving, will you?'

Rhianna nodded. 'I've already called them. They say there aren't any beds available at the moment.'

'Then ring them again and hurry things up. This man is a priority case. He needs to be admitted urgently.'

'I'll do my best.'

'When you've sorted that out, the woman in cubicle four needs attention.' His tone was sharp. 'She's been waiting for more than an hour to have her wound sutured.'

'I'm working as fast as I can,' Rhianna snapped back. 'I only have one pair of hands, or perhaps you hadn't noticed.'

'What I've noticed is a build-up of patients who need attending to right away,' he retorted. 'If we're landed with a major emergency on our hands in the next few minutes, we're going to be hard put to cope with it.'

'I don't believe that's my problem,' she answered with a bite. 'I'm doing as much as I can, as fast as I can. In the worst-case scenario, you'll have to divert people elsewhere.'

'That's not going to happen—not while I'm in charge, at least. If things get too bad, we'll have to call in agency help.'

A senior management official came over to intervene. Rhianna had seen him wandering about the department earlier and she had wondered why he was there. Perhaps he was checking up on how things were going.

'Could we calm things down here, do you think?' He looked from one to the other with cool grey eyes. 'You're all under pressure here, it's plain to see, but if we can't get waiting times down sufficiently, we'll have to think through our options.'

He glanced at Bryn. 'Getting agency help in is one alternative, but it's a costly one. In the meantime, it isn't going to help if tempers get frayed.'

He waved a hand towards the doctors' lounge. 'Perhaps the two of you should take a break and cool off a bit.'

He moved off, and Bryn muttered something under his breath. Rhianna thought it had something to do with management not knowing an emergency when they saw it, but she couldn't be sure and, anyway, she had the feeling that part of Bryn's curt manner was to do with their disagreement the other day. He was still angry with her because she had deceived him about being Nathan's mother.

She had never known him to let things concerning their work get on top of him, and his manner with everyone else in A and E was calm and even-handed.

It was she he had a problem with. Things were definitely not going well between them, and he had been terse with her on more than one occasion lately.

It was true that she was struggling to keep up with the demands that were being made on her, but she didn't think she was so far behind to be singled out.

'The stroke unit?' he reminded her caustically,

breaking into her reverie, and she jumped in startled acknowledgement.

'I'm onto it,' she said.

'Good.' His blue eyes ran over her assessingly. 'When you've done that, perhaps you should go and grab a coffee. I'll ask Dr Peterson to look at the suture.'

She didn't argue with him. She felt as though she was just about at the end of her tether, with the pressure of work and the worry over Gwyneth. Nathan had been feeling unwell, too, and she thought it might be through anxiety over his mother, although she couldn't be sure. She shielded him as much as she could, but he was an intelligent little boy and he didn't miss a lot.

An hour or so later, things had calmed down a fraction in the department, and she made her escape outside to her favourite place by the silver birch. Unfortunately, she discovered that Bryn was already there, and she came to a sudden halt, taken aback and wondering whether she should turn around and go back where she had come from.

'Wait,' he said, as she began to swivel around. 'You don't need to go. I was just about to leave.'

'You don't have to do that on my account.'

'I know.' He studied her, and she glared back at him defensively, her chin up, her green eyes sparking.

His expression was grim and it goaded her to say tautly, 'We ought to be able to work together without snapping at each other every five minutes, don't you think? People are beginning to notice the atmosphere between us and wonder about it.'

'I doubt that,' he muttered. 'If you think we've been tetchy with one another it's most likely all in your imagination. We've all been feeling the strain lately. There are too many patients and too few staff-grade doctors to go around. You said that was one of the problems before I started here. Things haven't changed a great deal since then.'

'Maybe not.' She looked up at him, hurt by the way he had distanced himself from her and not knowing how to put things right between them. 'I don't think I'm wrong about the way things have changed between us. You're angry with me. You have been angry ever since you found out that Nathan isn't my child.'

He returned her stare. 'All right, since you insist on bringing it up. I'll admit it. I'm disappointed that you could go on lying to me week after week. You did it so well, too.'

His mouth made a straight, hard line. 'Why did you lie to me about Nathan?' he asked. 'Did you think it would put a barrier between you and any man who might want to get close to you if you let it be known that you had a child? Were you trying to push me away?'

She shook her head. 'I don't need to put up defences, do I? Anyway, this wasn't about me.'

She was quiet for a moment. 'The truth is, I did it because you were getting to know Colin all over again and I thought you might let something slip to him about Nathan. Gwyneth doesn't want him to know that she had his child.'

'I may not approve of Colin's behaviour, but that's being unfair to him, don't you think?'

'No, I don't. He would never have been able to cope with having a son, even if he had wanted to. His life was a mess, and Gwyneth doesn't want Nathan dragged into that.'

'At some point he needs to be told. He should accept responsibility for fathering a child.'

'That isn't for us to say, is it? It's Gwyneth's decision to make, and she chose to keep it from him.'

'That was between you and Gwyneth. Why did I have to be dragged into the deception? You let me think that Nathan was yours. You made a fool of me.'

'I didn't want to hurt you in any way.' She gave him an anxious look. 'Believe me, I didn't want to deceive you, but I was afraid you would tell Colin the truth, either purposely or by accident.'

'Putting aside the fact that it might not have been a bad thing, did you really think I would go shooting off at the mouth about something that wasn't my concern?' His tone was scathing. 'Why would I do that?'

She made an awkward little shrug. 'I'm not saying that you would mean to do it, but these things happen. Anyway, you never had a high opinion of Colin, and in the past you sometimes let him know that you thought he should change his way of life, that he should accept responsibility as a married man when

Gwyneth was unhappy. I thought you might feel that he should be told about Nathan. I couldn't be sure what to expect. You're guided by your own set of rules.'

'I didn't tell him what he should do. I offered him advice when he asked for it, even if I didn't think he would take it. In his more reasonable moments he talked to me about his problems with Gwyneth and I told him what I believed to be right. I don't see any justification for you to lie to me because of that.'

'Perhaps I was wrong,' she admitted. 'I'm sorry if I offended you. I hadn't meant to attack your integrity, I was simply doing what I thought would be best for Nathan. Gwyneth was sick with worry that if Colin found out about Nathan he might demand custody of him while she was in hospital. I couldn't bear to see her making herself wretched when she needed to concentrate on getting well.'

He didn't look as though he was convinced by her argument, but he said coolly, 'How is she now? I know she was to have surgery on her heart valve. Has she come through that all right?'

Rhianna swallowed against a lump in her throat. 'The operation went well, but she's very weak still. We should have a better idea of how she's doing in a day or so.'

Bryn's glance moved over her. 'Let's hope she'll find the strength to get well again now that the infection's behind her. She's been ill for a long time. It must have drained her resources to the limit and beyond.'

He straightened and pushed himself away from the tree. 'I should get back to work,' he said. His jaw was hard-edged, and Rhianna was unhappy to see that his manner had not softened in any way. She had hoped he might find it in him to forgive her for what she had done, but it didn't look as though that was going to happen.

Back in A and E a short time later, things soon became frantic again. An accident at a factory had brought an influx of patients suffering from burns, and she was busier than she would have liked, but at least it kept her from dwelling on her own problems.

Later that day, just as she was about to go off duty, her father came by A and E and poked his head around the door.

'There you are,' he said with a smile. 'I was hoping I would catch you before you left.'

'And you did. I see you have Nathan with you,' she said, going over to him, her mouth curving, despite her weariness. Nathan peered around the door, following his grandfather's cue and not coming into the room.

It was her father's half-day at the pharmacy and he had promised to collect Nathan from nursery school, but he hadn't said anything about stopping by A and E. Seeing them both here now filled her with sudden misgivings. Had there been bad news about Gwyneth?

'Is everything all right?' She stepped out into the corridor.

Nathan beamed at her. 'We're going to see Mummy,' he said. 'Only for a little while, Gan'pa says, because she's still poorly.'

'That will be lovely for you, won't it?' she murmured.

He nodded. 'I told Gan'pa I wanted to come and he said, ''Yes, all right, then.''' He pulled a toy car from his pocket and began to race it along the wall, happy that everything was going his way and oblivious to the adults.

'I was hoping it would give you a bit of a break if I took him with me to see Gwyneth,' her father said.

Bryn came out into the corridor as he was speaking, and her father acknowledged him with a brief smile and a quick nod of the head before turning back to Rhianna.

'You've been looking exhausted lately, and I thought maybe I could take him out for a snack meal afterwards and then I'll bring him back to your house later. In fact, if you want to go out for a few hours yourself, that's fine by me. I know you haven't been able to get out and about on your own for some time, and I want to do everything that I can to make life easier for you. I can stay with him at the house until you get home.'

He looked at Bryn. 'Both of you are looking as though you've had enough.'

Bryn's mouth twisted. 'It's working here that does

it. We haven't even had a chance to get a proper lunch-break today with one thing and another.'

Howell was shocked. 'That's not good for either of you, is it?' He looked Bryn over. 'How can you go on working all day without adequate rest periods and a chance to eat a substantial meal? That's how people come to make mistakes.'

Rhianna had known for a long time that her father had a soft spot for Bryn, and he often asked what was going on in his life, how his career was going.

Bryn shrugged lightly. 'Sometimes it can't be helped. It's the way things go.' He gave Rhianna a dry glance. 'I suspect Rhianna thinks I'm working her too hard. She's been accusing me of giving her a hard time.'

Rhianna made a rueful face. 'I didn't say that, exactly. But it's true about the lunch-break. We were teeming with critical injuries that couldn't wait, and that can be very draining on the people who work in A and E, especially when we're short-staffed.'

Her father said, 'That's all the more reason for taking time out when you get the chance. You could always go and get something to eat now. There's a new place that's opened up on the waterfront. It overlooks the beach, and I've heard good reports of it. Haven't tried it myself, mind, but I'm told that they do excellent fish dishes and delicacies as well as more traditional fare.' He looked from one to the other. 'You both look as though you could do with getting away from here for a while.'

Rhianna pulled a face. 'Maybe, but I have a stack of ironing to do, among other things.' She glanced at Nathan, who had begun to make roaring sounds, imitating a jet aeroplane. He followed up the sound with his hand, directing it in an arc above the toy car, which was now scooting along the corridor. She had loved having him stay with her, but the downside was that there was so much more work to do, having a child to care for.

'Leave the chores,' her father advised. 'They'll still be there when you get home, but you might at least feel more like tackling them when you've had a proper break.'

'Eating out sounds like a good idea,' Bryn put in unexpectedly. He glanced at Rhianna. 'Perhaps we should do as Howell suggests. I don't know about you, but I'm starving, and I don't much fancy the idea of going home and having to cook.'

'There you are. It's as good as settled.' Her father looked pleased with himself, and Rhianna hadn't the energy to argue.

'I'm not sure I'm dressed for the occasion,' she said with a grimace. Her work clothes were nothing special, just a cotton top and a slim-fitting skirt, whereas Bryn always managed to look smart. He was wearing a beautifully tailored grey suit that looked well on him, and beneath the jacket he had on a dark-coloured shirt.

'You look just fine,' Bryn said. His glance skimmed over her, tracing the line of her figure-hugging top and the way the skirt curved smoothly over her hips. 'As Howell says, we could both do with getting away from this place for a while.'

After the terse exchanges that had gone on between them earlier, his manner now was brisk but perfectly reasonable, and she had no idea why he had made this sudden about-turn. If he was happy enough with the idea, it might not be a problem to go with him to the restaurant. It might at least give her the opportunity to try to put things right between them.

'Why not?' she agreed. She glanced quickly at her father. 'Will you tell Gwyneth that I'm thinking of her?' She doubted that she would be allowed to visit if her father and Nathan were going along. Too many visitors would tire her cousin.

'I will. Try to relax for an hour or so. It'll do you the world of good.'

She and Bryn arrived at the restaurant about a half an hour later. It was perfectly situated, as her father had said, overlooking the small bay, so that as they sat at a table by the windows and looked out, they could see the clear blue of the sea, its foamy waves lapping gently at the shore. The setting sun gleamed on the ripples of the water, casting a golden glow over everything.

Rhianna ordered a dish of pasta dressed with a sauce made from sun-dried tomatoes, along with a side salad, and Bryn settled for something more substantial in home-baked pie with potatoes and a selection of vegetables. They were both hungry, and ate with relish, their meal interspersed with light snatches of conversation.

There was still a slight awkwardness between them, but as time progressed Rhianna gradually began to relax. Bryn appeared to have put their differences to one side for the time being, Nathan was being looked after, and she was free from responsibility for a while. It was a refreshing feeling, and it was good to enjoy the simple pleasure of being waited on and tasting beautifully prepared food.

'Has there been any news about Colin?' Bryn asked as their desserts were brought to the table. 'He had a bad head injury, didn't he?'

'He's all right. He was concussed for a while, but there was no fracture, and they kept him in for observation because he was feverish. It was a virus of some sort that caused him to fall, but he seems to be over the worst now. He'll probably be able to leave hospital tomorrow.'

'It must have been a worrying time for you.' Bryn was watching her expression, his spoon poised over his apple crumble dessert.

'It was. When he went missing for a few days, I was afraid that he might have reverted to the lifestyle he had before, when he would go back on the drugs and drop out for days at a time. I didn't know what to expect when I saw him lying on the floor.'

'But he hadn't taken any drugs?'

She shook her head. 'No. The blood tests confirmed

that. He seems determined to put all that behind him now.'

'That must be a relief for you.'

'Yes, it is. I was worried at first, because he and I had talked and I think he had been upset by something I had said to him. I was afraid I might have pushed him into doing something foolish, but as it turned out he had gone away for a few days to think things through.' She tasted her fresh fruit dessert and it melted satisfyingly on her tongue. 'I think he might be turning the corner at last, and perhaps now he might be able to start afresh.'

'So, are you and he planning a life together?'

The question startled her. She stared at him, her green eyes puzzled. 'Why would we do that? I thought you understood... Nathan isn't my child. He's Gwyneth's son.'

'I know that, but you have always stood by Colin. You've always cared for him.'

'But not in the way you mean.' She frowned. 'I'm fond of him. I've always thought that he had the potential to be a good man, to get more out of life than to simply waste it on drugs. I thought I could stand by him and help him, but I don't love him.'

'You did at one time. You dated him for quite a while.'

'I was young then, and I didn't see beyond the brashness of youth. We went out together for a while, and we had some good times together. He made me laugh sometimes, and he helped me to get over my mother's death, but there were never any deep feelings between us.'

'But you were upset when Gwyneth married him.' Bryn sipped at his coffee, watching her over the rim of his cup.

'Because I thought he would hurt her in the end. I could see what was happening to him. He was dabbling in drugs and managing to hide what he was doing from most people, but he refused to get help and Gwyneth refused to see any wrong in him. It was a painful time for all of us.'

Bryn replaced his cup on the saucer, sat back in his chair and watched her for a moment or two, studying her features thoughtfully. 'I didn't realise that was how you felt. I thought you were in love with him.' He paused, his mouth making a wry shape. 'I must have hurt you by saying the things I did. I accused you of breaking up his marriage to Gwyneth, but you must have been simply trying to help him piece his life together again. I'm sorry.'

She shook her head. 'You don't need to be sorry. It's all water under the bridge now.' She was a little sad, thinking about the way things had turned out. She had never loved Colin. Her heart was reserved for Bryn, and she had loved him in secret for a long, long time, but it had never come to anything because he had only ever thought of her as a friend. He had gone away out of her life, to pursue his career, and in a month or so, when his time here came to an end, he would be moving on again.

She finished her own coffee and then glanced down at her watch. 'I should be setting off for home. I know my dad said that he would watch Nathan for me, but Nathan can be a little fractious at bedtime unless he's settled properly. All this worry over his mother has been upsetting for him.'

'I'll follow you home to make sure that you get back safely. There have been a few accidents along that back lane lately.'

'Mostly because people shoot out from the side turning. I think there are plans to make it safer. But thanks all the same.'

He followed her as he had said he would, and when she parked her car in the garage at the side of her house, she was surprised to see that he had stopped his own car on the drive, alongside her father's.

'I wanted to say that I'm sorry if I made life difficult for you at work these last few days,' he said, coming to stand beside her in the porch. 'I didn't mean for it to be that way. Blame it on pressure of work and problems with staff levels. I've been juggling rotas and when I should have been working I had to sit in on interviews for people applying for my own position at the hospital. If I've been harsh with you of late, it isn't because of anything that you've done. You're a good doctor. You work hard and you're compassionate and caring, and you have enough to contend with at home. You don't deserve to be put under pressure.'

'That's all right. I understand.' She looked up at

him with troubled eyes. 'So it's true that you'll be moving on soon, is it? Have you another place in mind?'

'I've put in applications at a couple of hospitals. There's one consultant post in Derbyshire that is quite appealing. It would mean more responsibility—a bigger department and more prospects for me, and it's a permanent position. I feel I'm ready for that now.'

'Have you heard anything yet?'

He shook his head. 'I've been for an interview, and I'm in with a good chance, but they have a couple more candidates to see before they make a decision.'

She was thrown by the news. It was only what she had expected, but all the same it was a blow to hear that he would be leaving the area. In her heart, she had hoped he would stay.

'So somebody new will be taking your place,' she said. 'I had wondered if they would make your position a permanent one. Bringing people in on a temporary basis is not going to be much use in the long term, is it?'

'Try not to let it stress you out,' he murmured. 'As you said this morning, you can only do so much, and it isn't your responsibility to worry about staffing levels and keeping the department functioning.'

He reached for her, his arms sliding around her waist, and she felt reassured to have him hold her once more. It seemed like an eternity since he had held her in his arms.

'You do a wonderful job,' he said, 'and you cope

the best way you can. You should take time to relax more often.' He smiled down at her. 'It was good spending time with you away from the hospital. You've had a lot to contend with lately and it was good to see you sit back and put your cares to one side for a while. I know you're going through a difficult time and I wish I could ease the burden for you.'

She looked up, wondering at the tenderness in his voice, and as she lifted her face to him his gaze lingered on her features, tracing the curve of her cheek in the shadows of the porch, and then moved down to linger on the softness of her mouth.

She wasn't aware of him edging closer, but he must have done because in the next moment he bent his head towards her and his lips were on hers, taking gentle possession of her mouth. He deepened the kiss with a soft sigh that rumbled in the back of his throat.

Or perhaps she was the one who was making muted sounds of need and longing. His hand was splayed out against the small of her back, bringing her up close against him, and her body flamed as his taut, masculine frame crushed her soft feminine curves. His strong thighs pressured her into the welcoming shelter of the porch, and she gave herself up to his kisses, returning them in full measure, exhilarated by the demands of his mouth and the way his hands were exploring her body.

'It feels so good to hold you this way,' he murmured against her lips. 'You're perfect, so warm and soft and feminine, so beautiful.' His breathing was laboured. 'I don't know how I've waited so long to be with you like this.'

'Bryn…do you really mean that?' She stared up at him, hardly daring to hope that it could be true.

'I need you,' he muttered, his voice thickened. 'I want you.'

His fingers lightly cupped her breast, and her whole body melted in sensual abandon. She wanted him, too, wanted this wonderful moment to go on and on. Through the fine cotton of her top she felt the heat of his palm, the way his thumb lightly stroked the aching nub of her breast.

She longed for more, enticed by the increasing boldness of his caresses as his hands trailed over her, smoothing over the curve of her spine, the swell of her hips and the line of her thighs.

A light came on inside the house, and for a moment she was confused, her senses reacting in bewildered chaos. At the back of her mind it finally registered that her father must have switched on the hall light.

'Bryn…the light… My dad is there with Nathan…'

'I'd almost forgotten.' His hands had been caressing her just a moment before, and now he let go of her, and she stared up at him, her mind disorientated, her nervous system still raging with the memory of his kisses and his gentle exploration of her body.

He drew back from her, and she felt isolated, as though a cold draught of air had wafted over her. 'I have to go,' he said quietly. 'I'll see you at work tomorrow.'

'Yes. At work.' She watched him turn and walk back to his car, and she put her fingers to her lips as though to remind herself that his kisses had been real. More than anything, she wanted to be with him, to have him kiss her again and hold her as though he would never let her go, but reality was beginning to creep in.

He wanted her, he said, but he had told her that he was going after a job that would take him a couple of hundred miles away from here. How could she bear it if he was to leave her?

It was bound to happen at some point. He wanted the extra responsibility, the potential for promotion that the job offered, and he would be the ideal candidate for it, she knew. He was so experienced, so well qualified, and they would be foolish to turn him away.

She had always known that his career was tremendously important to him. She would come a poor second place next to that. If he didn't take the consultant's post in Derbyshire, there were bound to be others.

Inside, her heart ached because he couldn't possibly love her as she wanted to be loved. He didn't care enough, and the wound that knowledge made on her would never heal. It would stay with her for ever.

CHAPTER NINE

'WE'RE going to lose this patient unless we can get his heart rate to slow down,' Bryn said. 'It's way too fast, and his temperature is through the roof. Let's give him dantrolene and metoprolol IV. They might do the trick.'

Rhianna was deeply worried that their patient wasn't going to pull through. It was the weekend, and she was working the late shift with Bryn. These were the early hours of the morning and alongside seriously ill patients they were having to deal with all the injuries that had come about when young men staggered out from nightclubs and picked fights while they were stoked up with alcohol.

Those cases all had to wait when Alec had been brought in. He had collapsed at a disco, and his friends had driven him to hospital as quickly as they could, but he was in a bad way.

Rhianna had started to work on him straight away, and at least she had managed to secure the young man's airway, but she was alarmed by the way his condition was fast deteriorating.

'Has he taken any drugs?' Rhianna asked, but his friends shuffled and hung their heads and had been hesitant to give her any information.

'I can't treat him properly unless I know what it is that he's taken,' she said urgently. 'We don't have time to mess about. If you want to help him you must tell me everything you can, quickly.'

'He had some Ecstasy tablets on him at the disco,' a girl offered diffidently. 'I don't know how many he took. I saw him take one, but he may have taken another later on.'

The group of teenagers were restless, shocked by Alec's collapse, and they were beginning to get in the way when Rhianna was doing her best to treat him. Emily swiftly ushered the friends out.

'Could just one tablet have had this effect on him?' Rhianna asked Bryn.

'It's possible,' he answered. 'The drug may have been contaminated. Anyway, he may have been using Ecstasy on a regular basis, and repeated use could have caused damage to his liver.'

Rhianna was in a quandary. Everything they tried seemed to be failing, and it was heart-rending to see such a young man carelessly throw his life away.

'Nothing's working,' she said, under her breath a short time later. 'His pupils are dilated and the hypertension is off the scale. Shall I try nifedipine?'

Bryn nodded. He was working fast alongside her, doing everything he could to save the youth's life, but Alec was convulsing, and things were looking bad for him.

They struggled on, but it was almost an hour later before Alec's condition began to stabilise. Rhianna was feeling drained, and Bryn said, 'You should go and take a break. There's nothing more we can do for him right now.'

She nodded, but her expression was bleak as she looked at Alec. 'Do you think he'll come out of this unscathed?'

'He may do. He's young and strong and, provided that he doesn't go on abusing his body, he may be all right.'

Bryn glanced at her searchingly. 'This happened to Colin once, didn't it? He was brought into hospital and almost died, but he came through it in the end.'

'That's true. I think he must have reached rock bottom and decided that he had to fight his way back up. I don't think he'll ever go back to how he was.'

'So you have faith that he'll recover well enough to be told about his son?'

'I don't know. That isn't my decision to make.'

'But it might be. Have you thought about what will happen if Gwyneth doesn't get back on her feet? She's asked you to take care of Nathan, hasn't she? What would you do then? Would you tell Colin the truth?'

Rhianna was pensive. 'I'll deal with that situation if it happens. I hope it won't come to that.'

He didn't press her any more on the subject, and she was relieved about that. It wasn't something she wanted to dwell on.

'Are you going to visit her today? You said your

father wasn't able to spend much time with her last night because she was so weak.'

'I want to go and see her later on, and talk to the doctor if I can, but I'm not sure what to do about Nathan. My dad has to go out and I don't think I should take Nathan with me. It might be upsetting for him to see her like that...'

'I could look after Nathan for you, if you like,' Bryn said. 'He knows me and we seem to get along all right together these days. I could take him along to the playroom here at the hospital and keep him amused while you go and visit.'

'Are you sure you don't mind?' It was an offer she was all too happy to accept. It meant that she could find out about Gwyneth's well-being without worrying about Nathan at the same time.

'I'm sure. I told you that I'd do anything I can to help out.'

'Bless you. I'd really appreciate that.' She smiled at him, her heart filled with love and warmth for him. 'You're being very good to me.'

He returned the smile. 'You're more than welcome.' He gave her shoulders an affectionate squeeze and looked down at her with eyes that gleamed and spoke volumes. She suddenly wished that they weren't in a busy emergency room with people rushing here and there all around them. More than anything, she wanted him to hold her and cherish her and soothe away all her worries and fears in the way that only he could.

It was the middle of the afternoon when she finally managed to see Gwyneth, but her condition had not improved much and she was still sedated after the operation. Rhianna sat quietly by her bedside and held her hand for a while and all the time she was willing her to get well.

Gwyneth stirred once or twice, but barely managed a smile, and Rhianna left a while later with a heavy heart.

She went in search of Bryn and Nathan and found the child sitting at a table in the hospital's playroom, constructing a castle from plastic bricks.

'Hello, chick,' she greeted him, making an effort to put on a cheerful face. 'Have you been having a good time in here while I've been away?'

He was strangely subdued and simply shrugged his shoulders without answering. Her glance flew to Bryn.

'He doesn't seem like his normal self,' she said in an undertone. 'Has something happened?'

'He hasn't said very much, so I can't be sure what he's thinking,' Bryn answered, 'but I think he's had a bit of a shock. We went to get something to eat from the snack machine, and while we were there we ran into Colin.'

'Colin? What was he doing there?'

'He was discharged from the hospital this afternoon, and he came to the machine to get himself a drink before he left for his flat. We stood and chatted together for a few minutes.'

Rhianna's heart began to thud. 'What did you chat about?'

'This and that.'

'I don't understand,' Rhianna said, her alarm growing. 'Nathan's clearly upset about something. What aren't you telling me? What happened?'

Bryn hesitated, and her glance went to Nathan. The little boy was frowning, carefully putting the last plastic block in place. Then he stood up and said, 'Can we go now?'

'Yes, of course,' she said. 'Nathan, what's the matter? Has something upset you?'

He shrugged again. 'Don't know,' he mumbled. Then he looked at her, his grey eyes clear and trusting, and said, 'Have I got a daddy? A real daddy?'

Rhianna frowned, not knowing what to say, but Nathan went on, 'Bryn said that man was my daddy, but I don't know him. Him and Bryn talked, and the man said to me that he was my daddy, but I never seened him before. I don't want him to be my daddy.'

Rhianna didn't answer him straight away. She couldn't speak. She was shocked to the core that Bryn would betray her that way, knowing how much it meant to her that Colin didn't hear the truth just yet. It had made no difference to him in the end, though, how she felt, and he had gone ahead anyway and told Colin and then he must have confronted the child with it.

She turned to Bryn, her face shuttered, her eyes shards of ice. 'How could you?' she said in a voice that was barely audible. 'How could you do such a thing?'

Bryn started to speak, but she wasn't listening. She held out her hand to Nathan and said, 'I'll talk to you about it in a little while. Let's get away from here and go home, shall we? You can tell me all about it when we get there.'

Hurrying away from the playroom with him, she didn't stop and look back. She was aware that Bryn was saying something to the nursery nurse in charge, and she guessed that the girl had asked him to sign the register to confirm that Nathan was leaving. Rhianna was glad that he was delayed. It gave her the opportunity to get out of there unhindered.

Nathan was confused, naturally. He had discovered the news about his father in a totally unprepared way, and as a four-year-old he didn't know what to make of it. She had her work cut out to explain to him why he hadn't seen or heard of his father before today, and when she had finished she couldn't be sure that he fully understood what she had said.

'Your daddy was poorly when you were born,' she told him. 'He was ill for a long time, and that's why he didn't know about you. He was too poorly to come and see you.'

'Is he better now?'

'I think so.'

'So Mummy will get better as well? She's been poorly for a long time.'

Rhianna hugged the boy to her. 'I hope so, chick. I hope so.'

She felt sick inside. Why had Bryn done this? She had felt so close to him these last few days, and even if he was going away she could have held him in her heart, knowing that he cared. But now he had destroyed all that.

Worse still, she didn't know what Colin was going to do with the information that he had a son.

She put Nathan to bed later that evening and tucked him in with his teddy bear cuddled to him. 'Goodnight. Sleep tight,' she said, kissing him.

Luckily he fell asleep fairly quickly, and she went downstairs to tackle a few chores. When the doorbell rang, she hesitated, wondering if it was Bryn, but after a moment or two she got a grip on herself and went to answer it.

Colin was waiting on the doorstep, looking grey-faced, his eyes dazed-looking as though he, too, was still in shock.

'I need you to tell me that it's all true,' he said. 'I've discovered that I have a son, Nathan. Gwyneth never told me about him and it's all come as a huge shock to me. Why didn't she tell me about him?'

Rhianna swallowed hard. 'Come through to the living room.' She ushered him along the hallway and invited him to sit down. It was plain to see that he was devastated by the news.

'She didn't tell you because she didn't believe you would be able to be a father to him,' she said flatly.

'When she discovered that she was pregnant, you had already left her. At that time you weren't able to hold down a job, or even live a day-to-day life without getting yourself in a mess. You could go for days, weeks at a time and be oblivious to everything. That's why she kept it from you. She thought it would be for the best if she brought him up on her own.'

'I still can't take it in,' he said thinly. 'She kept it from me. All this time, I had a son and I missed his formative years.' He looked at Rhianna, his eyes wide and uncomprehending. 'How could she do that to me? I know I was a mess, but I could have changed. I could have been a father to him.'

Rhianna shook her head. 'I don't think you could, Colin,' she said gently, 'not then. You were too steeped in your way of life. It wouldn't have worked out.'

'Is he here? Can I see him?'

'He's asleep. He's had a difficult day, and I don't want to disturb him.'

'But I could look at him, couldn't I? I want to see him again, Rhianna.' There was a firmness in his tone that made her wary, but she decided that it might cause more problems in the long run if she didn't agree to his request.

'You're not to wake him,' she warned him. 'I don't want him to be upset. He's had enough for one day.'

'I won't do anything to upset him,' he said, but she went with him all the same and stood by as he stared down at the sleeping child.

He was very quiet, very still, just watching him, and finally, after several minutes, he turned and walked out of the room.

Downstairs, he said, 'I'm going to make sure that I'm acknowledged as his father. He's my son, and I should have been told about him.'

Rhianna tried to talk to him about the consequences, but she could see that he wasn't really listening to her. He had made up his mind, and there would be no stopping him.

She let him out of her front door a few minutes later, troubled by what he had said. The last thing Gwyneth needed right now was trouble from Colin and who could tell whether he could sustain his recovery from his drug habit? How would Nathan fare if Colin decided, after telling Nathan he was his dad, that it was all too much for him and he succumbed to drug abuse once more?

Some half an hour later the doorbell rang again, and Rhianna braced herself to answer it. What now?

It was Bryn. 'Don't shut me out, Rhianna, please,' he said. 'I need to talk to you. It's important that you listen to what I have to say.'

'Why is it? Are you here to defend what you did? What gave you the right to interfere, to tell Colin what Gwyneth had kept from him?'

'I didn't tell him.'

Her eyes widened in disbelief. 'Do you really expect me to believe that?'

'It's the truth. Let me come in and give me the chance to explain.'

She didn't see how he could explain away his actions, but she held the door open and let him in. Perhaps she should hear him out, and then she could let him know what she thought of his actions and in some small part she might rid herself of this awful feeling of betrayal that threatened to eat away at the heart of her.

They went into the living room and she stood by the window, too restless to sit, too angry with him to relax her guard.

'I didn't tell Colin about Nathan,' he said. 'I thought he should know, but I wasn't the one to tell him. He found out completely by accident.'

Her eyes blazed at him scornfully. 'Do you really expect me to believe that?'

'It's the truth.' He came over to her and looked at her steadily. 'I took Nathan to the snack machine, as I said, and Colin came along. He had been on the ward that was just off the corridor from the machine. It was totally by chance that we had gone to that particular machine—the one on the same floor as the playroom wasn't working.'

He pulled in a deep breath. 'Anyway, Colin and I talked for a while, passing the time of day, and I asked him how he was getting on, what he was doing there. He said he had just come from the ward, where they had discharged him just a few minutes earlier. The doctor had said his fever had gone and his concussion had cleared and there was no reason to keep him in any longer.'

'So how did the question of him being Nathan's father come up?'

'A nurse came from the ward to tell him that she had forgotten to give him a letter for his GP. She handed it to him and then she looked at Nathan and then back at him and she said how much alike they were. She said she hadn't realised that he had a son. She said they were like two peas in a pod, except that Nathan's hair was a little lighter than his.'

Rhianna gasped. 'What did Colin say?'

'Nothing, just then. I think he was too stunned for words. He mumbled something and smiled at her and took the letter, and she went back to the ward. Then he looked at Nathan and said, "You must be about four years old. That would be about right. Your mother and I were good together for a while, but then it all went wrong. I must have left without knowing that she was pregnant."'

'So you're saying that he worked it all out for himself?'

Bryn nodded. 'He did. Then he asked me outright and I tried to fudge the issue, but he wasn't having any of it. He said it had all started to fall into place.'

Rhianna looked at him anxiously. 'Bryn, I'm sorry that I doubted you. I should have known. I should have had faith in you.'

He drew her to him, his arms closing around her. 'It's all right. I understand how you must have felt. I wasn't sure how to handle it at first, but when we came away Nathan was asking so many questions that I felt I had to tell him the truth. I didn't mean to hurt either of you.'

'Oh, Bryn, we've made such a mess of things between us. Colin wants to be acknowledged as Nathan's father. What are we going to do?'

'I'll talk to him again, and try to get him to see sense. I may be able to get him to accept that he could have access, provided that it's supervised for the foreseeable future.'

He bent his head to hers and kissed her gently on the mouth. 'I wish that I could take care of you, take all your worries away. I know how anxious you are about Gwyneth. If I could make it all come right for you, I would.'

He stroked her cheek lightly, and then kissed her again, harder this time, possessively, as though he would make her his own and shield her from everything that threatened to harm her.

'I'm glad that you're here with me,' she said raggedly. 'I need you to be with me, Bryn. I feel so lost without you.'

'I'm here. I need you, too. I love you, Rhianna. I think I've always loved you. I know that I want you more than anything in the world.'

'Do you?' She said it in a whisper, not daring to believe that it could be true.

'I do, believe me.'

He loved her. It was what she had longed to hear

and now his words filled her with joy. There was nothing more she wanted either, except to have him here with her, holding her as though he would never let her go.

He drew her down on to the settee and sat beside her. He kissed her thoroughly, throwing her senses into feverish chaos, easing her back against the cushions and running his hands over her as though he would discover every part of her.

She trailed her fingers over his face and moved against him, her body meshing with his, yearning for something more.

'I've wanted you for so long.' He breathed the words against her heated flesh.

'I want you, too.' She said it in a muffled whisper, but it was as though she had lit a fire in him. His kisses were pure flame, burning with passionate intensity.

He said softly, 'I tried not to let you know how much I cared, because I believed you only had thoughts for Colin. I've wasted so much time.'

'Bryn…' His name was a sigh on her tremulous lips. 'I love you. Don't you know that? I've always loved you.' The blood was racing through her veins like a tidal wave, her heart crashing with love and desire at the same time.

It was all he needed. His lips tasted her, trailed over the softness of her curves and lingered for a breathtaking eternity. 'I've been such an idiot.'

She reached up and touched his face once more with her fingers, memorising every line, every contour.

She wasn't sure how it happened, but after that they somehow ended up in her bedroom, and he was laying her back against the quilt, his hands caressing her, seeking out all her hidden places, making her feel more feminine than she had ever felt before.

He looked down at her and his breath seemed to catch in his throat. Slowly, gently, he began to ease the clothes from her. With equal desire, she slid her hands beneath his shirt and ran her fingers over his velvet-smooth skin.

His kisses were hot and tantalising, and she returned them in full measure. Shakily, her fingertips moved over his chest, outlining his tautly muscled frame, gliding over the flatness of his stomach and revelling in the smooth warmth of his skin. Beneath her hands she could feel the thunder of his heart, thrashing in time with her own.

She had hardly dared dream that this would ever happen, but when he moved over her and they were suddenly as one, she knew that this was everything that she had ever wanted.

The rhythmic movements of his body stirred a tumult of passion in her, and she was suddenly overwhelmed by the clamour of her senses, desire lifting her to a crescendo of desperate need, where she was seeking some unknown, elusive fulfilment.

Then, all at once, in an eddying whirlpool of sensation she was flung onto the crest of a wave, which crashed and tumbled and filled her whole being with joy and contentment.

At the same time it seemed as though Bryn's whole body shook with intense pleasure. A groan shuddered in his throat, echoing his convulsive, pent-up release.

Afterwards Rhianna felt as though she was slowly floating back down to earth, and for the first time in her life she was complete.

His breathing came in ragged spurts, and he shifted slowly, lowering himself beside her. Kissing her tenderly, he looked down at her. 'Are you all right?'

She smiled up at him, her gaze still dreamy with the embers of spent passion. 'More than all right,' she said softly. 'And you?'

'On top of the world.' Heat glimmered in his blue eyes. 'That was the most incredible experience,' he said, his voice thickened.

'I thought so, too.' Her mouth was softly curved, relaxed in a hazy, blissful world where nothing could invade her peace and happiness.

They lay together, slowly drifting back to normality. Then, after a while, he sat up and began to pull on his clothes.

He made a faint frown. 'I should have asked about birth control. I was in such a hurry, and I didn't give it a thought.'

'There's no need to worry about that,' she murmured. 'I take the pill.' All the same, she was suddenly a little cautious. Had she let herself be carried away too easily? He had said he loved her, but now he seemed to be having doubts about what they had just done. 'Are you sorry about what happened?'

'No, never.' He dropped a kiss on her mouth. 'It's just that there's this job in Derbyshire to consider. If I have to go away, I don't want to leave when there might be the possibility of repercussions.'

'Are you going away?' A wave of panic suddenly washed through her. 'Did you get the job?'

'I was offered it, yes.' He searched her face. 'Will you come with me? I want you to be with me.'

She stared up at him, her eyes troubled. 'I can't.' All at once her hopes were dashed, as though icy droplets of water were dripping down on her, washing away her chance of happiness.

'Are you absolutely sure about that?' He was watching her closely, his expression sober. 'I had to leave you before, when I was first starting out as a doctor. I needed to expand my horizons, but it would have been selfish to ask you to sacrifice your own career for me. You were so young, and you were about to start medical school, and I couldn't drag you away from that. But things are different now.'

'You didn't tell me that you felt that way.' She looked up at him in bewilderment.

'I couldn't bring myself to do it. It wouldn't have been fair to you, but I hoped that if I came back when you were more settled, things might be different.' His face was sad. 'Then, when I came home for a break, I saw that you were dating Colin. Every time I saw you with him I wanted to say that you were making a mistake, that he wasn't right for you, but then you went back to medical school and we went our separate ways again.'

'You had it all wrong. There was never anything serious between me and Colin.'

'I know that now. But back then I felt that I had left it too late. You were making a life for yourself, and I wasn't part of it.' He cupped her face with his hands. 'Can't we change all that now? Will you think again about coming with me? There will be other jobs for you now that you're qualified. Doctors are always needed in A and E…but this position would be special for me. I would be in charge of a larger department, there would be more staff and it would be a step up for me. Will you think about it?'

She pressed her lips together to stop them from trembling. 'It isn't as simple as that. I have to think about Gwyneth and Nathan, and my father. I can't just leave them.'

'Nathan could come with you. Not now, of course, but later…if it should turn out that way. Neither of us wants to contemplate that, but if things turn out for the worst, and Colin decides he doesn't want custody… He likes me, and I could be a father to him.'

She shook her head. 'I can't do that to him. It would mean taking him away from everything that's familiar to him, from his friends and his grandad.'

She blinked away the tears that threatened behind her eyelids. 'Besides, I think Gwyneth will get well again. I need to believe that, and I know that she'll need me to be close at hand once she's home. My father needs me, too. He doesn't say as much, but I know that he wants me to stay nearby. He and Gwyneth and Nathan are the only family I have, and they're precious to me. I want to be with you, but I couldn't leave them.'

She was heartbroken, having to say that to him, but she didn't see any way around the situation. She wasn't a high flyer, a woman in search of career prospects or someone who was anxious to discover new places. She was a home bird, a nest-maker, and she knew she would be deeply unhappy if she were to be torn from her roots.

'I'm sorry. I should have known better than to ask. I wanted you to be with me. We've been apart for so many long years and I hoped that now all that separation might come to an end.'

'It's what I want, too, but I don't see any way out. Above all, Nathan needs me right now, and he needs to be here, near his mother, with everything and everyone who is familiar to him. I can't tear him away from all that.' She looked up at him, tearfully. 'You do understand, don't you?'

He nodded. 'I understand.' He stood up and made an attempt at a smile. 'I have to go. It's late and I'm dead on my feet and I have to be up early in the morning for a series of meetings. I'll see you at work.'

She made to get up off the bed, but he gently pressured her down. 'Don't get up. I'll see myself out.'

He went downstairs and let himself out of the house and Rhianna buried her head in her pillow and cried herself to sleep, knowing that he was moving on, preparing to go out of her life once again. She felt utterly miserable.

In the morning, she showered and dressed for work and tried to put on a cheerful front for Nathan. The little boy was jumping about, asking about his mother, wanting to know when he could go and see her.

'Perhaps later on today, after nursery school,' she told him. 'It depends how she is. She may not be well enough to see visitors.'

'She will. I know she will.' Nathan wasn't going to be put off. 'Mummy will want to see me. She said I was her bestest boy.'

'Of course you are. She loves you loads, you know that, don't you?'

He nodded. 'So you'll take me to see her?'

'All right,' she promised. Even if he had to look at her through the window of the little ward, she would let him see her.

She didn't see Bryn at all that day, and she guessed that he must be attending the meetings that he had talked about. Was one of them in Derbyshire? Her stomach was heavy, as though it was lined with lead.

There was good news to come, though. Gwyneth was sitting up in bed when she went to see her with Nathan, and there was colour in her cheeks and a liveliness about her eyes that Rhianna had not seen in a long time.

'You look so much better,' Rhianna said in astonishment. 'Do you feel any better?'

'Like a new woman,' Gwyneth said. She put her arms around Nathan and hugged him close to her. 'They say if I keep on getting stronger, I might be able to come home quite soon. I might need to convalesce for a while, but I should make a full recovery.'

'Oh, Gwyneth, I'm so happy for you. That's wonderful news.'

'It is, isn't it? I told Uncle Howell, and he said he was going to put banners out. I told him he'd better not. I don't want any fuss.'

'I don't think we'll be able not to make a fuss. It's so good to see the change in you.'

Gwyneth reached out and held Rhianna's hand. 'Thank you for taking such good care of Nathan for me while I've been ill. I don't think I could have got through this without you.'

'I wanted to help,' Rhianna said. 'You're like a sister to me, and I need to know that you and Nathan are all right.'

She wasn't going to tell her about Colin, and she didn't think Nathan would blurt anything out. He was too busy telling his mother about the things going on at nursery school and about his friend's birthday party.

'They had balloons and prizes and they all went to the farm and had rides on the tractor,' he told her excitedly. 'Can I do that on my birthday?'

'I should think so,' Gwyneth said with a smile. 'It isn't for quite a while yet, though, and I know I'm going to need Rhianna to help me organise it.'

'It's in the bag,' Rhianna said, and Nathan giggled.

'That's silly,' he said. 'You can't put a tractor in a bag.'

She was showing a cheerful face for both their sakes, but when she went back home at the end of the day and thought about going on without Bryn as part of her life, she felt as though she had walked into an impenetrable fog. It was a bleak prospect and, no matter how glad she was to see that Gwyneth was on the mend, her heart was aching to be with Bryn.

He came in to work next day, and said quietly, 'Can we go outside and talk for a while? There's something I need to say to you, and I don't want you to hear it third hand.'

Her heart sank. Was he going to tell her that he was leaving within a day or so? Wouldn't she even have time to prepare herself?

They went and stood outside by the silver birch. They were working the late shift again and the afternoon was almost finished. The sun was beginning to set on the far horizon, though it was still warm. A few birds were still chirruping from the trees all around, but mostly everywhere was quiet except for a faint breeze rustling the leaves.

'What did you want to say to me?' she asked softly. 'Is something wrong?'

'No. Nothing's wrong. I went to see Colin yesterday and we talked for a long time about what he planned to do, and after a while he said he understood why we were all worried about him storming ahead with everything. He said that he'll take things steadily. He's going to wait until Gwyneth is fully recovered, and then he wants to ask if she'll allow him to see Nathan from time to time so that they can get to know each other. He doesn't want to hurt Gwyneth or Nathan, and he feels that he owes it to them to do things properly. I believe he'll keep to what he said.'

Rhianna let out a sigh of relief. 'I'm glad about that. It wasn't what I expected, but you must have talked him round. It's good news.'

'Yes, it is.' He glanced at her questioningly. 'Have you seen Gwyneth? How is she?'

'She's much better than I could have hoped for. I'm thrilled to bits that she's looking so much stronger. I'm sure she's going to be all right.'

He smiled. 'Good. That's brilliant news.'

Rhianna sent him a quick glance from under her lashes. 'Is that what you wanted to see me about? Colin and Gwyneth?' From his manner she had wondered if there was something more, and she hardly dared breathe in case what was coming was going to be too hard to bear.

'I wanted to tell you that I've turned down the Derbyshire offer.'

She stared at him, wide eyed. 'You turned it down? But I thought it was what you wanted?'

'It was a great opportunity, but I couldn't accept it, knowing that you weren't going to come with me. I've accepted a permanent post here at this hospital, and I hoped that it would mean that you and I could be together.'

He reached for her hands and held her lightly, watching her face for signs of her reaction. 'Will you marry me, Rhianna? I couldn't bear to lose you all over again. I want you to be by my side for always. I want us to be man and wife, and have children if it's possible, and stay together until we grow old. What do you say? Will you be my wife?'

Her lips curved in a smile. It felt as though the sun had come out in full force and was sending out a promise of happiness that would last for ever, and when she looked at the horizon and the setting sun, she saw that the sky was filled with a golden glow.

'It's what I want, more than anything,' she said softly, looking into his eyes. She went into his arms and nestled against him, and when he claimed her mouth once more, they sealed their love with a kiss that promised they would be together for the whole of their lives.

RP MEM/MED

WE VALUE YOUR OPINION!

YOUR CHANCE TO WIN A ONE YEAR SUPPLY OF YOUR FAVOURITE BOOKS.

If you are a regular UK reader of Mills & Boon® Medical Romance™ and have always wanted to share your thoughts on the books you read—here's your chance:

Join the Reader Panel today!

This is your opportunity to let us know exactly what you think of the books you love.

And there's another great reason to join:

Each month, all members of the Reader Panel have a chance of winning four of their favourite Mills & Boon romance books EVERY month for a whole year!

If you would like to be considered for the Reader Panel, please complete and return the following application. Unfortunately, as we have limited spaces, we cannot guarantee that everyone will be selected.

Name: ______________________________

Address: ______________________________

______________________ Post Code: ______________

Home Telephone: ______________ Email Address: ______________

Where do you normally get your Mills & Boon Medical Romance books (please tick one of the following)?

Shops ❑ Library/Borrowed ❑

Reader Service™ ❑ If so, please give us your subscription no. ______________

Please indicate which age group you are in:

16 – 24 ❑ 25 – 34 ❑

35 – 49 ❑ 50 – 64 ❑ 65 + ❑

If you would like to apply by telephone, please call our friendly Customer Relations line on **020 8288 2886**, or get in touch by email to readerpanel@hmb.co.uk

Don't delay, apply to join the Reader Panel today and help ensure the range and quality of the books you enjoy.

Send your application to;

The Reader Service, Reader Panel Questionnaire, FREEPOST NAT1098, Richmond, TW9 1BR

If you do not wish to receive any additional marketing material from us, please contact the Data Manager at the address above.